"Your body is lovely— and I should know."

Farrah shivered at the seduction in Joel's voice as he went on. "I wanted you that night. A fleeting emotion but true nonetheless."

Disbelieving, she stared into the sleepy passion of his narrowed eyes. "You wanted me?" she repeated tremulously.

"Yes." His hand covered the nervous movements of hers. "Does that surprise you? It shouldn't." He smiled mockingly. "I don't usually make love to women I find unattractive."

She gasped. "But you didn't make love to me!"

"No, but I could have. It was too soon, that's all. It wasn't the right time for us."

"It will never be the right time!" Farrah cried indignantly. "I won't be *used* in this pretense!"

CAROLE MORTIMER
is also the author of these

Harlequin Presents

Many of these titles are available at your local bookseller.

For a free catalogue listing all available Harlequin Romances and Harlequin Presents, send your name and address to:

HARLEQUIN READER SERVICE
1440 South Priest Drive, Tempe, AZ 85281
Canadian address: Stratford, Ontario N5A 6W2

CAROLE MORTIMER

only lover

Harlequin Books

TORONTO • LONDON • LOS ANGELES • AMSTERDAM
SYDNEY • HAMBURG • PARIS • STOCKHOLM • ATHENS • TOKYO

Harlequin Presents edition published May 1982
ISBN 0-373-10502-9

Original hardcover edition published in 1979
by Mills & Boon Limited

CHAPTER ONE

JOEL looked up with a scowl as the intercom buzzed on his desk. 'Yes?' he asked curtly, his soft American drawl only faintly discernible.

'Your eleven o'clock appointment has arrived,' came Cathy's smooth reply.

Again Joel scowled. He wasn't in the mood for being pleasant this morning; last night's scene with Laura was still too vivid in his mind for him to be feeling polite. He clicked on the intercom again. 'Show them in, Cathy,' he said with a sigh.

His dark mood didn't lift as Cathy opened the connecting door between their offices to usher in the person waiting to see him. Cathy smiled at him before leaving the room, closing the door softly behind her. Joel transferred his attention to the girl who had entered the room at Cathy's bidding.

He needed no more than his normal male instincts to tell him that here was a beautiful girl. Her hair was a beautiful golden cap, wavy tendrils at her forehead and nape giving her the look of a cherub. But the tall curvaceous body certainly didn't belong to a child, far from it. The clear green eyes surrounded by thick dark lashes and the creamy matt complexion perhaps had too much of a look of forced innocence for Joel's liking, but if she could carry it off with any degree of conviction, who could blame her for trying? And the innocence did look natural, it was only Joel's cynical disbelief of all women that told him otherwise.

Joel sat forward in his deep leather armchair. 'What can I do for you——' he consulted his appointment book. 'Miss Halliday?'

Farrah licked her lips nervously, moving forward over the scatter rugs to stand in front of the huge mahogany desk. The desk seemed to be the only concession made to this room being an office. Huge leather-bound books lined the walls, deep leather armchairs in a rich brown colour stood either side of a huge drinks cabinet that looked, and probably was, a genuine antique, and half a dozen scatter rugs littered the highly polished floor. To Farrah it was like stepping back into the early nineteen-hundreds, and she felt even more unnerved than she had sitting outside in the reception area.

Joel Falcone was perhaps the only modern thing about this room and yet he wasn't in the least reassuring, with his dark over-long hair tinged with grey at the temples and shaped into the nape of his tanned neck, a hawk-like nose and firm sensuous lips that were now set in a straight forbidding line. But it was the eyes that affected her the most, narrowed icy blue eyes that appeared to miss nothing, and she was sure they didn't. His charcoal grey suit fitted perfectly across his powerful shoulders and the silk shirt gleamed whitely against the darkness of his skin.

'Well, Miss Halliday?' he said tersely, his voice deep and husky.

'Don't you——Don't you know me, Mr Falcone?' she asked tremulously.

He raised an arrogant eyebrow. 'Should I?'

'Perhaps not me, but perhaps P-Paul Halliday.' The last came out breathlessly.

Joel's dark brow creased in thought. 'Paul Halliday,' he repeated slowly. 'You're his daughter? Or perhaps his wife?'

'His daughter,' she admitted. Still she saw no dawning comprehension in his dark arrogant face. 'Don't you know who my father is?'

Joel began to feel impatient. He couldn't be bothered with this guessing game. 'As far as I am aware your father works in the accounts department,' his eyes sharpened with interest. 'Ah, I begin to understand. Your father stole from this firm, did he not? Are you here to plead on his behalf?' he mocked cruelly.

'Not plead, no,' her eyes sparkled angrily. 'And my father did not steal from you. He borrowed a small amount of money and——'

A deep mirthless laugh interrupted her tirade. 'Your father did not *borrow* anything. And it was hardly a small sum. Twenty-five thousand pounds taken systematically over eleven months could hardly be classed in that light.'

Farrah's hands wrung together and Joel was forced to notice what beautiful hands they were, long and tapered with perfectly lacquered nails. 'But my father *needed* that money. Oh, I know that doesn't excuse him, but you wouldn't miss twenty-five thousand pounds among your millions.'

'Maybe not, in fact, I'm sure not,' Joel said blandly. 'But the excuse that he needed the money is hardly my affair. For whatever reason he stole that money, gambling debts, drink—although if he used all that money on drink he would be in his grave by now, or even if it was to buy you out of trouble, I do not see why my company should bail him—or you—out.'

She bit her lips hard to stop them from trembling. Her father had warned her that Joel Falcone was a hard man, but she hadn't realised just how hard. She had come here today with the intention of begging if necessary, but she couldn't do such a thing before this hard unyielding man. He would merely look down his nose at her and not give an inch.

'He didn't need the money for himself—or me for that matter. I have no need of money.'

Joel looked at her elegant summer dress, her sheer tights and the well fitting leather shoes. His eyes moved slowly back to her face, and once again he was struck by her beauty. 'I can see that. Do you have yourself a rich middle-aged protector who tries to live through your youth?' he said this with a sneer, and Farrah flinched at his contempt.

Two angry spots of colour appeared on her creamy cheeks and suddenly she looked very youthful, her eyes wide and distressed. 'I don't have a rich protector, Mr Falcone,' she told him stiffly. 'You just happen to pay well.'

'*I* do?' For once his bland expression deserted him. 'Do you work for me?'

'In Angie Preston's department,' she supplied unwillingly, the last thing she or her father needed was for her to lose her job too. At the moment she was supporting both of them, although how long she could continue to do so she wasn't sure. The Falcone newspaper and magazine organisation did pay well as she had said, but certainly not enough to support two people.

'The problem page!' he said with disgust. 'And how long have you been with the firm?'

'Three years now, ever since I left school.'

'School?' Joel echoed sharply. 'How old are you?' he asked.

Farrah hesitated. She had deliberately dressed to look older for this appointment today, although with these baby waves that was quite difficult. And now she had ruined it all with a slip of the tongue. 'Nineteen,' she supplied miserably.

Joel's eyes narrowed even more. 'And what does a child like you hope to achieve by coming here to see me? Your father is an embezzler and must pay the penalty for such a crime.'

'Oh, but I'll—I'll do anything to save him from going to prison,' her eyes pleaded with him. 'Anything!'

'Don't you think that's rather a rash statement to make, Miss Halliday?' he said coldly. 'You don't know what manner of man I am. I could ask anything whatsoever of you and you would be compelled to comply.'

'Oh, but I—you wouldn't——' She blushed fiery red.

'You're right, I wouldn't.' His lips curled with distaste. 'At thirty-seven I'm nearly as old as your own father. I haven't taken to seducing babes, no matter how charmingly they offer themselves to me. Does your father know what you're doing?'

'He knows I've come to see you, yes.'

'Why couldn't he come himself?'

'He isn't well,' Farrah replied resentfully. 'He couldn't go to prison, Mr Falcone, it would kill him. Please don't prosecute him!'

Joel began to look bored. 'The prosecution of your father is not my concern. I have security people to deal with things like that.'

'Please don't be so cruel, Mr Falcone. My father is a sick man, and this worry isn't helping him. He stole that money for a good reason, I promise you that. I'll pay it all back, really I will.'

He gave a harsh laugh. 'Twenty-five thousand pounds! My dear girl, you may only be nineteen, but it would take you nearly a lifetime to pay me back on the salary you earn.'

'I don't intend to be working on the problem page the rest of my working life. I want to be a proper journalist.'

'It would still take you years.' He became thoughtful, his dark face almost satanic in its intensity. He might be thirty-seven years of age, but he was certainly the most excitingly handsome man Farrah had ever seen. He was like a sleepy feline, sleek and beautiful, and just as dangerous. She watched him as the silence continued, wondering what he was thinking behind that enigmatic expression.

'You could just be the answer to my problem,' he spoke softly, so softly she could hardly hear him. Joel looked at her critically. 'A little young perhaps, but that can't be helped. At least you're beautiful.'

'What are you talking about, Mr Falcone?'

He smiled slightly, but it was a smile without humour. 'Just an idea I have. You said you would do anything—I hope you meant that. Go now, I have to think this over.'

'But I—I—— When will I know?'

'When I damn well choose to tell you,' he snapped. 'I'll call you in the department tomorrow. I take it you will be in to work tomorrow?'

'Yes, but I——' She could just imagine the girls' astonishment and curiosity if she were summoned up to the fifteenth floor to see the owner, Joel Falcone. She was only a very junior member of staff while this man was the owner of newspapers and magazines both in England and abroad, and was never seen by his minions. None of the girls in her office knew anything of her father's embezzling—she cringed at the word, but in truth there was no other description more fitting —they all assumed he was ill. How could she explain the reason for Joel Falcone's summons without involving her father?

Blue eyes narrowed to icy slits. 'I care nothing for your embarrassment,' he guessed the reason for her silence correctly. 'Just make sure you come when you're called.'

Farrah could do nothing else but accept his words as a dismissal, he was obviously a man of forceful character who didn't expect his words to be questioned. Miserably she made her way home. She had thought she would be able to give her father some good news when she returned, but she was to be disappointed, and so, unfortunately, was he. The interview hadn't yet been concluded.

Her father looked up expectantly as she quietly entered their flat, his green eyes so like her own looking at her avidly, almost eagerly, and what he read in her face made his shoulders droop unhappily. Farrah could cheerfully have hit Joel Falcone's arrogant face at that moment for causing her father this extra pain.

'No luck, I see,' said her father wearily.

She sat down beside him on the sofa, taking his painfully thin hand into her own, trying to give him some of the warmth she had felt from the blazing sun outside. She smiled at him reassuringly. 'It will be all right, Daddy, really it will.'

'I bet the arrogant devil wouldn't even let you through the door when he realised who you were.'

Farrah couldn't bear the look of defeat on her father's face, a man who had once been a tall proud man, now but a shrivelled shell of himself. 'You're wrong, Daddy, I did see him. We talked for about ten minutes or so.'

'But you didn't get him to stop prosecution did you?'

'Well no, but I——'

'Typical Italian is Joel Falcone,' mumbled her father. 'Not an ounce of forgiveness in their body. Just pure revenge.'

Farrah attempted a light laugh, but her father's words had sent an icy shiver down her back. 'He isn't pure Italian, Daddy—well, not really. He's an Italian-American, he's probably never even been to Italy.'

'Of course he has, Farrah, he has a branch of Falcone's over there. So he wouldn't agree to drop the charges,' he repeated.

'I didn't say that, Daddy,' she licked her lips nervously. 'He hasn't made up his mind yet.'

Her father looked at her sharply. 'What does that mean?' he asked slowly.

Farrah stood up to pace the room, a large sun-filled room that seemed to reflect her mother's own sunny personality. God, she missed her mother! What would she have done in this situation? What a stupid question that was; if it weren't for their love of her mother this situation wouldn't have arisen. But neither of them had realised her father was stealing that money. She forced a cheerful smile. 'I'm to go back and see him tomorrow.'

Paul Halliday looked at her suspiciously. 'What for?'

'I don't know, Daddy. Just to give me his answer, I suppose.'

'He could have done that today. He didn't make a pass at you, did he? I've heard of his reputation with women and it isn't very flattering. He had a string of women before finally settling for Laura Bennett a few years ago. Not that he's changed much. There seem to have been just as many women, and she isn't much better.'

'No, Daddy, he didn't make a pass at me. Far from it. He told me he was old enough to be my father.'

'And so he is. Must be forty if he's a day.'

'He's thirty-seven, actually. And he's rather handsome in a dangerous sort of way. He's not the ordinary type of man you see about. There's something sort of— well, sort of *special* about him. You know—he's the sort you could never ignore in the street,' she bubbled over with laughter. 'He looks as if he should be the head of the Mafia or something, with all that black, grey-sprinkled hair, that dark harshly handsome face and the expensive handmade suits.'

'Don't even say things like that in fun, Farrah. You never know.'

'Don't be silly, Daddy. He doesn't look the violent type—powerful, yes, and seemingly completely in control of his own destiny, but not physically violent, at least, not needlessly so.'

'He made quite an impression on you, didn't he, child?'

'Oh yes. He was—well, he was quite something. Frightening, but so very much alive. He seemed to emit suppressed power, as if it only needed some little thing and he would explode into life. But he's cold—so cold, as if love has never touched him, or he has never allowed it to. It's strange really, I only saw him for a few minutes and yet I can remember him vividly.'

'Now then, Farrah,' her father said briskly, 'don't become fanciful about the man. Remember, my future depends on him.'

All the light died out of her face as she sat down again beside her father. 'Don't worry so, Daddy,' she hugged him. 'Everything will work out, you'll see.'

She told herself the same thing many times over the next day, looking up nervously every time the telephone rang. She had wanted to wear something rather smarter than the fitted denims and checked shirt that she usually wore, but that would have only drawn attention to herself. And that she could quite well do without. Especially after this morning's conversation with Fiona.

Fiona had sat on the side of Farrah's desk, a tall leggy brunette who was aware of her own beauty without being conceited. She was very popular with both sexes and Farrah returned her smile companionably. 'Something wrong?'

She referred to the letters she had just passed on for reply to the older girl. Fiona shook her head. 'No, these are fine. It's just that—well, you were off sick yesterday, right? Well, I could have sworn I saw you in the building,' she looked puzzled. 'In fact I thought you were going up in the private lift to the fifteenth floor.'

'Who, me?' Farrah did her best to give a teasing smile, she only hoped Fiona was convinced by the shaky result. 'Going up to Joel Falcone's office? You must be joking!'

Fiona stood up, smiling self-derisively. 'I thought I must have been wrong. None of us ever see the great man. I've never set eyes on him, and I've been here nearly four years.'

'Rather elusive, is he?'

'Elusive! The man's positively unattainable.'

'But he's very friendly with Laura Bennett,' Farrah pointed out, 'so he can't be that unattainable.'

'His sleeping partner, in more ways than one,' scoffed Fiona. 'I've always said business and pleasure shouldn't be mixed, and they're a good example.'

Farrah looked up now as Tracy beckoned her to the internal telephone. 'Joel Falcone's office,' she said in awed tones.

Farrah quickly took the receiver, turning away from the several pairs of eyes that had turned to look at her at Tracy's outburst. 'Yes?' she said breathlessly.

'I want to see you now,' came the cool clipped tones of her employer.

'Now?' she repeated stupidly.

He gave an impatient sigh. 'Now, Miss Halliday, don't keep me waiting.' The telephone clicked down firmly at the other end.

Farrah looked about her awkwardly, quietly making her excuses to leave the office before the girls' curiosity got the better of them and they actually started to ask questions. She almost ran out of the office, getting into the lift and pressing the button for the fifteenth floor. Her heart began to beat erratically, sounding like a bass drum to her ears. The procedure of yesterday was repeated, except this time she wasn't kept waiting but was shown straight into Joel Falcone's spacious office.

Again as yesterday, he was seated behind the huge imposing desk, but dressed less formally, the dark grey business suit of yesterday discarded in favour of a black silk shirt opened casually at the neck and black trousers that fitted closely to his long muscular legs.

His eyes narrowed appraisingly as he took in her own appearance and Farrah put up a nervous hand to ruffle her short cherubic hair. It was an endearing gesture, and made those icy blue eyes narrow even more.

'Miss Halliday,' he said deeply.

'Mr Falcone,' she replied huskily. 'I—er—— You asked me to come.'

'Of course I did, Miss Halliday, I'm not so ancient that my memory fails me,' his mouth twisted mockingly. 'We have a conversation to finish.'

Farrah blinked nervously. 'Yes, Mr Falcone. You—um—you said you had something to think over.'

Joel Falcone stood up, his tall lean frame even more intimidating as he came round the desk to stand in front of her. 'Won't you sit down, Miss Halliday?'

She looked round at the leather armchair just behind her, dropping down thankfully into its luxurious depth and then wishing she hadn't as she realised how much smaller it made her feel as she looked up at him.

He began to pace up and down the office, emanating a completely masculine aura as he occasionally looked at her before turning frowningly away again. Suddenly he stopped in front of her. 'Tell me, Miss Halliday—what do you think of me?'

Farrah looked at him open-mouthed. Whatever it was she had been expecting it certainly hadn't been a question like this. 'Wh-What do I think of—of *you*?' she asked hesitantly.

Icy blue eyes pinpointed her to the chair and Farrah

moved back involuntarily. 'Yes, *me* Miss Halliday, not Joel Falcone your employer, but Joel Falcone the man.'

What on earth was he talking about? Farrah felt completely bemused. She didn't quite see what this conversation had to do with her father and the taking of this man's money. 'I don't quite see ...' She shook her head.

'No one is asking you to. Answer the question, Miss Halliday.'

Farrah looked at him closely to see if he was mocking her, but his expression was unreadable. What could she say about such a man, especially to his face? Her cheeks blushed a fiery red and she sat forward uncomfortably. 'Well, I—I don't know what to say!'

'The truth would perhaps be preferable,' he drawled dryly. 'Speak up, girl. I don't bite—well, not babies like you anyway, and certainly not in these circumstances.'

She blushed again, looking away from his taunting face. 'What am I supposed to say? You know what you look like, so why ask me?'

Joel Falcone sighed in exasperation. 'I don't mean my physical looks—well, perhaps I do, but I don't mean the fact that I have dark hair, am tall, of Italian descent from my skin colouring, and look my age. I want to know how you feel about *me*, how my looks affect you?'

'Well, for a start you don't look your age, experienced and—cynical and——'

'Yes? Well, don't stop now. This conversation could be the deciding point of your father's immediate future.'

'Oh! Oh well, in that case,' she looked at him critically. 'You're cynical most of all—and rather condescending. And arrogant. But you're attractive too.'

'Oh, I'm glad about that,' he interrupted mockingly. 'Let's concentrate on that, shall we?'

'All right. Well, you have a sort of magnetism, animal

magnetism I think they call it. And your features are ruggedly attractive, not handsome, you understand, but very attractive.'

Joel Falcone walked back around his desk and sat down again, smiling slightly at her embarrassment. 'So we have established that you don't find me repulsive. That's good—in the circumstances. And I—*I* don't find you repulsive either. Too young for my taste, but then only I know that.' He was talking quietly to himself again. He looked up at her. 'Sorry, honey, I was far away.'

Farrah shrugged her shoulders. 'What's all this about, Mr Falcone? I don't understand you.'

'No, I don't suppose you do. But you will—oh, believe me, you will. Do you know anything about my personal life?'

She hadn't, but during the last twenty-four hours she had learnt that he had more than just a business relationship with the other owner of this firm, the actress Laura Bennett, but they both had other relationships. She paled. Surely he wasn't interested in her that way? Hadn't he said she was too young for him? But he had also said she wasn't repulsive to him. When she said anything yesterday she hadn't meant *anything*!

'Relax, Miss Halliday. And as you don't seem to have an answer I will assume that you have heard a little about me but don't feel able to reveal it,' he laughed harshly. 'Why you should feel so reticent I have no idea. You've already called me cynical, condescending, and arrogant, so why draw the line at my private life?'

Her green eyes sparkled at his intended mockery. 'I said those things because I know them to be true. The things I've heard about your private life are exactly that, hearsay. I don't feel able to judge you on that.'

Joel Falcone's mouth tightened visibly and Farrah flinched from his icy gaze. 'I'm not asking you to *judge* me on anything,' he snapped coldly. '*You* are hardly in a position to judge anyone.'

Farrah sprang agilely to her feet, sparks of anger shooting from her eyes. 'You're cruel, Mr Falcone!' she choked.

He smiled, a slow leisurely smile that taunted and mocked. 'Yes, I'm that too. Sit down, Miss Halliday,' he said harshly, all humour leaving his face to be replaced by a cold mask. 'You asked for my help when I would be quite happy to let the law deal with your father. I thought I had found a way to help him and myself at the same time. It seems I was wrong.' He stood up in conclusion of the interview. 'You wouldn't be co-operative, and a sulky angry companion I can do without.'

All anger left Farrah at his dismissive words and her shoulders slumped dejectedly. She dropped back into the chair. 'Please, Mr Falcone, I—I didn't mean to lose my temper. If you have some way of helping my father then I'll gladly help—co-operate, whatever,' she said anxiously.

'You really are desperate, aren't you? Very well, we'll get back to my private life. You have no doubt heard of my long-standing friendship with Laura Bennett.' His mouth curled back sneeringly as she blushed. 'I thought so, it seems to be public knowledge, wouldn't you say?'

'Yes,' she agreed softly.

'Yes. Well, up until now it has been a very—*intimate* relationship, shall we say? Yes, very intimate.' Joel Falcone obviously felt no embarrassment at his conversation, but Farrah blushed fiery red. 'I see you understand my meaning,' he taunted. 'And while Laura may be satisfied with that sort of close business and personal arrangement, I find that it no longer suits me at all.'

Farrah felt tempted to ask what this had to do with her, but she resisted. She daren't anger this man any further. 'Yes?' she prompted.

He sighed deeply. 'So, I'm completely bored by the whole tedious affair.'

'Then why carry——? Sorry,' she bowed her head, 'I didn't mean to pry.'

'Why carry on,' he finished for her, feeling none of her embarrassment. 'I've asked myself the same thing many times. I don't have an answer—except perhaps that Laura seems to deliberately ignore any hints I may give about breaking up our relationship. At the begining I needed a hostess, I entertain a great deal, and I suppose you could say I used her. But whereas the affair seems to have cooled on my side, Laura seems determined to make something more permanent out of it. Needless to say, I don't want that. I want her out of my life once and for all.'

'Mr Falcone, I don't see why I need to know all this. It isn't any of my business, is it?'

'I'm not in the habit of telling my private affairs to complete strangers, in fact I don't discuss them with anyone,' his voice was bitingly precise. 'Unless of course I have a reason for it, and in your case I do.'

'And what is that?' Her curiosity was fully aroused now.

'It's quite simple really, Miss Halliday. As I've said, my affair with Laura is over as far as I'm concerned, at least in the physical sense, but she seems to want to carry on with it. It's come to the point where I don't even want to see her.'

Farrah was still puzzled. 'If you feel that strongly about it why don't you just tell her how you feel?'

'I've tried, but unfortunately Laura feels that her shares in this company give her some sort of special privilege where I'm concerned. They don't. I want to buy her out, but she seems to feel that if I did that she wouldn't see me again. She's right. I don't appreciate her using our business tie to force our personal relationship. I intend showing her that I don't need her—in *any* way. We have an agreement in our contracts that if either of us decides to sell, shares must be offered to the other partner before being put on the open market. I want to make Laura so mad she *has* to sell. Now this is where you come in. If Laura genuinely believes me to be in love with, and possibly contemplating marriage with, another woman, then she'll realise I mean what I say about severing our friendship. Her pride won't stand for too much of that sort of treatment. I wanted things to end differently, but she's made that impossible. So,' he sighed, 'in return for dropping the charges against your father *you* are going to become my much-loved girl-friend.'

CHAPTER TWO

'I'M *what*!' At his words Farrah had jumped to her feet and she stood staring at him with disbelief on her face.

'Calm down, Miss Halliday,' he said with infuriating calm. 'I realise my idea isn't quite what you expected, but——'

'You're right, it isn't!' Farrah burst out indignantly, glaring at him defiantly as she saw anger spark in those icy blue eyes at her interruption. 'How dare you!' she continued angrily. 'How dare you suggest such a thing? I couldn't do it!' she said determinedly, her tiny nose wrinkling with distaste.

'I said calm down, Miss Halliday,' Joel Falcone said without emotion. 'My suggestion that you do this for me was not meant in the physical sense. I've already said you're too young for my tastes.'

'Yes. Yes!' Farrah replied impatiently. 'But if you didn't mean for me to—to——'

'Go to bed with me,' he supplied tauntingly.

'Yes, go to bed with you! If you don't want that how will she ever think you're serious about me? That seems to be the normal way you progress.'

Blue eyes narrowed to suspicious slits. 'Do you *want* to share my bed?'

'Certainly not!' But the question gave her a warm unfamiliar feeling inside. What would it be like to be held in this man's arms? To be held intimately against his taut naked body? She brought her chaotic thoughts to a halt, her eyes opening wide with shock as she realised how wanton her thoughts had become. 'Then I don't understand,' her eyes were wide with bewilderment.

'This is all to be pretence, Miss Halliday. Just a way

of getting Laura out of my life.'

'I still don't see why you can't just tell her how you feel.'

'I've tried, damn you! She still maintains the mistaken idea that those shares give her some sort of hold over me, another woman should convince her otherwise. Although I doubt if she'll be very happy about it, especially as her rival is so much her junior.'

He said all this with a certain amount of satisfaction and she realised he was so angered by Laura Bennett's behaviour that he would enjoy doing this to her. 'I'm not her rival,' she said quietly.

'Only you and I will know that. As far as everyone else is concerned we'll be ecstatically in love with each other.' His mouth turned back in a sneer.

'Not if you act like that they won't.'

'Don't worry, Farrah Halliday, my acting will be superb.'

Farrah started shaking. This man really meant what he was saying! 'You can't really mean to do this, Mr Falcone——'

'Joel, please. If I'm to be your lover——'

'You aren't!' she said sharply.

'Your *pretend* lover,' he amended mockingly. 'Then you should call me by my first name.'

Farrah laughed brokenly. This couldn't be happening to her! 'No one's going to believe this, Mr Falcone —Joel then,' she said at his dark look. 'No one who actually knows us, especially Miss Bennett.'

'They'll believe it,' he said firmly. 'If you don't know that then you must be as innocent as you look, which no one could ever be. All those baby waves and trusting green eyes!' he said in disgust. 'What do you imagine all the girls down in your office are thinking at this moment? Well, I'll tell you. They probably think I'm making love to you right now. According to rumour, no woman is safe left alone with me.'

'They—they wouldn't think that,' she denied uncertainly.

'Sure they would. Why not? You're beautiful, in a childish sort of way. And like I said, no woman is considered safe alone with me.'

'But they wouldn't——' she shook her head.

'Of course they damn well would! And to convince them even more you're going to leave the building with me right now.'

'I am not!' Farrah said indignantly. 'It's only three o'clock. I can't just leave without telling anyone where I'm going.'

'I don't intend that you should. That wouldn't benefit us in any way.' He pressed down the intercom. 'Cathy, get me Angie Preston.' He turned to Farrah again. 'This should set the tongues wagging.'

'What do you mean to do——?'

The telephone buzzed to interrupt her and Joel Falcone picked up the receiver. 'Angie? Joel Falcone,' he said shortly. 'No, no, it isn't that. We'll get together about that some other time. I just wanted to tell you that Farrah Halliday won't be back in the department today. No, she isn't ill,' his eyes silently mocked her. 'She happens to be leaving with me.'

Farrah almost got up and ran then. It had started already, this deception that would become more and more involved. And she hadn't even agreed to it! But she had no choice in the matter. Joel Falcone had her trapped, and he knew it.

'That's right,' he continued, seemingly unaware of Farrah's inner turmoil. 'And she may be a little late in the morning too. Right. We'll talk about that other matter at a later date.' He rang off.

Farrah's eyes filled with unshed tears. 'This is terrible,' she said huskily. 'I can't go through with it.'

'Wouldn't you rather it happened this way than to have everyone know your father is nothing but a common thief?'

'He isn't a common thief! He needed that money, desperately.'

'So you've told me. I'd be interested to hear the reason.'

Anger sparked swiftly at his taunting voice. 'Well, you aren't going to. My father is twice the man you'll ever be. And do you know why? I'll tell you why. Because he loves. You couldn't love anyone or anything—you wouldn't know how to. But my father would and does, and for someone he loves he's willing to do anything. You're just a machine, Mr Falcone, a cold unfeeling machine!'

'But a rich one,' he said dryly, completely unmoved by her outburst. 'And in this case it means I hold all the right cards. Wouldn't you agree?'

'I hate you, Mr Falcone. I hate you!'

'No, you don't, Farrah. From this moment on you're going to love me, or at least pretend to. It's something I've found women are good at.'

'I couldn't even pretend to love you,' Farrah said hotly. 'You're hateful!'

'So you would prefer that I prosecute your father?'

'No! You know I wouldn't,' she said miserably.

Joel Falcone sighed impatiently. 'You can't have it both ways, you know. Go through with this pretence and I drop the charges against your father, plus forget the twenty-five thousand pounds he owes me. You know the alternative.'

'You consider this *charade* worth twenty-five thousand pounds!'

He nodded. 'I simply don't want Laura involved in my business affairs any longer. No doubt she'll want more than the market value for those shares.'

'And won't you mind paying it?'

He shrugged. 'Why should I? She'll be out of my life, finally.'

'That's some friendship you have there,' she said dryly.

'That's right, but I've just explained that to you.' He stood up in one fluid movement. 'Are you ready to leave now?'

Farrah also stood up, moving jerkily to the door. 'My—my bag and jacket. I left them in the office. I can't just leave them there.'

'That's all right. Angie wanted to talk to me about something anyway. You can collect your things while I talk to her.'

'Oh, but I——'

'Do it, Farrah!' he ordered impatiently. 'Make your mind up to this, because once we step outside this room there'll be no turning back. Once you're committed you will follow this through to the end. And no one is to know it's pretence. You understand, no one! Not even your father.'

'But I have to tell him,' she said, horrified. 'I can't let him think that I——'

'Not even your father, Farrah!' he repeated firmly. 'You can tell him when it's all over and not before. It shouldn't take long, a couple of months, no more.'

'A couple of months!'

He looked at her with steady blue eyes, collecting a burgundy-coloured leather jacket from what appeared to be a cloakroom and shrugging his powerful shoulders unhurriedly inside. 'A couple of weeks would hardly be convincing. The first few weeks we'll just make sure we're seen together in all the right places, later we'll progress to the occasional night spent together at my apartment.'

Farrah looked at his open-mouthed. 'I couldn't do that! What would everyone think if I stayed at your apartment? What would my *father* think!'

'Exactly what they're supposed to, I should imagine. Believe me, Laura won't be able to stand too much of that sort of treatment. She likes to think that any man she wants will come running when she calls.'

'But you won't,' she derided.

'Not any more—if I ever did.'

'You aren't the faithful type at all, are you?' she saw his mouth tighten angrily. 'I'm sorry, but you did say I wasn't to be sulky and angry.'

'I didn't say you had to be rude instead. And no, I'm not the faithful type. I've yet to meet a woman who can make me feel possessive enough to feel the need to be a one-woman man.'

'You consider women are only to be used and not loved?' she asked interestedly.

He gave a mocking smile. 'Oh, I *love* them.'

Farrah blushed. 'I don't mean physically.'

'I know that,' he smiled at her embarrassment, a mocking smile that taunted. He shrugged. 'No woman has ever proved to me to be any different, you're all money-grasping. A present pays for many things, but without them you get nothing.'

Farrah shook her head. 'That isn't true, at least not on my part. No man has ever given me presents for services rendered.'

Joel Falcone's eyes raked mercilessly over her casual appearance. 'Seeing you dressed like that, I can believe it.'

'Well, you don't exactly look the part of the debonair millionaire yourself,' she retorted tartly.

'Perhaps not,' he agreed. 'Okay, let's go.' He put a casual arm about her slim shoulders and felt her stiffen. 'Once we step outside this door,' he reminded her.

Farrah forced herself to accept his touch, resisting the impulse to move away from the closeness of his lithe athletic body. Not that it was unpleasant—that was the trouble. She found him much too attractive and dangerous this close to. And if his acting proved to be as superb as he said it would be she hated to think what would happen. His hand rested lightly on her shoulder and she could feel his warmth through her thin cotton shirt.

Those compelling blue eyes looked into her own apprehensive green ones. 'All right?' he asked softly.

'All right,' she agreed.

Joel Falcone opened the door for her, ushering her out of the office before him but managing to retain his hold on her. 'Smile, Farrah,' he said quietly. 'I don't want Cathy to think I'm taking you out of here under duress.'

Farrah forced an almost natural smile on to her lips, all too much aware of the vital man at her side. His secretary, Cathy, glanced up from her typing to look at them, her eyes narrowing with surprise as she saw her employer's arm draped casually across Farrah's shoulders.

'I'll be out for the rest of the day,' Joel Falcone informed her smoothly. 'Cancel the rest of my appointments for today, and for tomorrow morning.'

'Yes, sir.' Cathy looked puzzled by this strange turn of events. 'Is there anywhere I can reach you if necessary?'

Joel looked at Farrah. 'Under no circumstances am I to be disturbed,' he drawled. 'By anyone.'

Farrah walked out of the office with him, not having said a word, and the smile seemed fixed on her face. And this was just the start! 'I'm not sure I can go through with this,' she said shakily, moving away from him as they entered the lift together.

'Too late,' he said unconcernedly.

'Has it ever occurred to you that I might have a boyfriend?' she asked resentfully.

'It did, but no protestations were forthcoming in that

direction, so I assumed there wasn't a particular man in
your life.'

'But there is!'

'Then he can't be very important to you or you
would have mentioned him earlier. Forget him.' He
waited for her to precede him out of his private lift on
to the sixth floor. 'I already have.'

'Are you always this dismissive of other people's happiness?'

'Only when it's interwoven with mine. Look, Farrah,
no one is going to be hurt by this pretence of ours.
Laura just has a thing about becoming my wife at the
moment. Once she realises it's no go she'll be glad to
accept the money I'm offering her for her shares. Your
father will stay free, you will have whatever I care to
give you in presents during the next couple of months,
and I—well, I will gain my freedom from a determined
woman.'

'And how do I tell Nigel I won't be seeing him any
more?'

'That's up to you.' He stopped outside the door to
her department. 'I'll be with Angie only a matter of
minutes, join us when you've collected your belong-
ings.'

Joel Falcone caused quite a stir when he walked into
the large open plan office that accommodated ten girls
and Angie Preston who had her own separate office at
the end of the room, but when Farrah followed him in
all conversation ceased altogether and nine pairs of
eyes were riveted on them.

'I won't be long,' Joel said huskily, but loud enough
for people close to them to hear.

Farrah walked quickly to her desk, her head downbent as she gathered up her black velvet jacket and her
denim shoulder bag. This was proving to be more embarrassing than she had imagined and she could hear

a few whispers from her workmates now. Well, this was
no good, she couldn't creep about like this all the time,
and so flinging back her head almost defiantly she faced
the girls in the office with pride and dignity. Fiona was
looking at her with puzzled eyes and somehow Farrah
managed to summon up a smile.

Fiona came over to her. 'What's going on?' she asked
curiously.

'I—er—I—It's rather awkward to explain——' She
spotted Joel Falcone out of the corner of her eye as he
made his way across the office to her side.

He smiled straight into her eyes and Farrah felt her
heart lurch. It was a warm possessive smile and she
couldn't help but respond to it. She didn't think this
pretence was going to prove too difficult if he smiled
at her like that too often, in fact it could prove too easy,
much too easy, and it could end with her being very
hurt by this man.

'Ready to leave, honey?' Again his arm slipped about
her shoulders.

Farrah ignored the audible gasps coming from
around the room. She nodded. 'Ready,' she agreed.
'I'll talk to you tomorrow, Fiona.'

Complete silence followed their progress out of the
room, but as soon as the door closed behind them Farrah could hear the sudden murmur of conversation.
Joel Falcone gave a satisfied smile. 'By five o'clock this
evening the whole building should know about our
little affair.'

Farrah pressed the lift button for the ground floor.
'I don't see what good that's going to do, except embar-
rass me, of course. Miss Bennett is a famous actress, she
doesn't go about gossiping with the staff.'

'From little acorns ...' he quoted softly. 'The more
people who know about it the better. This way it will
be more believable.'

'If I don't believe it I don't see why anyone else should.'

'They will.' He studied her intently for several seconds. 'Of course you don't look kissed as you ought to do,' he took a step towards her, 'but that can soon be remedied.'

'No!' Farrah backed away from him, more frightened that he might get a response than of the actual man himself. 'I—I don't want to be kissed!'

He watched her through mocking eyes. 'Why not?' he asked softly.

'Because—well, because I—I don't find you attractive.'

'But you've already told me that you *do* find me attractive,' he reminded.

'I find a tiger attractive in the same way,' she retorted hotly. 'All right to look at from afar but too dangerous to touch.'

'Dangerous?' he repeated curiously. 'What a strange word to use!'

'But fitting, don't you agree?'

'Maybe.' He opened the lift doors with the touch of a button. 'Try to look as if you aren't terrified of me— or I could just give you that kiss here in reception.'

'You wouldn't!' Her green eyes widened.

'I wouldn't count on it,' he said lazily, retaining a tight hold on her arm as they walked unhurriedly out of the building. A black Ferrari stood parked on the forecourt and Joel Falcone nodded dismissal of the commissionaire as he moved to open the doors for them. Joel himself saw Farrah seated in the passenger seat before climbing in beside her. 'Comfortable?'

Farrah shifted about in the confines of the car, all too much aware of the man at her side. She could smell his aftershave and the clean male smell of him and her senses stirred unbidden. It was a fantastic car and completely suited to its sleek, confident owner. 'Fine, thanks,' she answered shortly.

'Good.' He put the car into gear.

'Where are you taking me?' Farrah asked with more confidence than she felt.

'Home,' Joel Falcone drawled. 'Your home.'

'Oh, but I thought——'

'I'm well aware of what you thought. I'm taking you home now and calling for you later. We're going to a nightclub I know.'

Farrah was completely fascinated by the harsh face of Joel Falcone, harsh and cynical and yet completely riveting. Deep lines of experience were etched from nose to mouth and his mouth had a cynical twist to it. He left her breathless and it took all her strength to answer him. 'Tonight?' she squeaked, swallowing convulsively at the thought of spending the evening with him.

'Sure, tonight.' Those deep blue eyes raked over her pale face, eyes surrounded by thick dark lashes that should have looked effeminate but didn't. 'You weren't going anywhere else, were you?'

Farrah gave a wan smile. 'If I were I'm sure you would tell me to break it.'

To her surprise he smiled too, a warm natural smile that reached his eyes. 'You learn fast, young Farrah Halliday. Were you going out?'

'No,' she admitted reluctantly.

'Then you won't need to break it, will you. Are you going to tell your father about me? Oh, not of our agreement, but that we'll be going out together.'

'Not until I have to.' She blushed as she realised how bad that sounded.

Joel Falcone frowned heavily. 'Do you think that's wise? It could come as quite a shock to him to learn from someone else that his little girl is having a full-scale affair with someone like me. If he's as ill as you say he is then the knowledge can't be going to help him.'

'Exactly,' Farrah said dryly.

'And it will be even worse coming from a stranger, or worse still, a newspaper. And how will your mother feel about it?'

It was a perfectly natural question in the circumstances, and yet Farrah felt a sharp pain at his casually spoken words. 'My mother is dead,' she said quietly. 'And I hope you'll leave it to me to tell my father.'

'I have no intention of seeing your father, when and how you tell him is up to you.' He stopped the car before the block of flats where she lived with her father. 'Can you be ready by eight-thirty?'

'I should think so,' she laughed lightly. 'It's only four o'clock, it doesn't take me four and a half hours to get ready. What—what do you want me to wear?' His steady gaze unnerving her and she fidgeted unnecessarily.

'We'll be going to a nightclub, quite an exclusive one. Do you have anything suitable?'

'Yes,' she snapped, stung by his condescension. 'Don't worry, I won't disgrace you.'

'I've arranged for you to go to a salon tomorrow and choose a new wardrobe. That's the reason I told Angie you would be late in the morning.'

'I don't want anything like that from you,' she told him angrily. 'I can buy my own clothes, thank you.'

'I'm sure you can. Consider these part of your payment.'

'I don't want anything from you,' she repeated firmly. 'Not your expensive presents or your clothes. Letting my father go free will be enough. And I can promise you that I'll pay as much of your money back as I can.'

'Did you know your eyes flash in the most tantalising way when you're angry?' he said huskily, ignoring her outrage and fiercely spoken words.

Farrah blushed fiery red. 'Don't prevaricate,' she said stiffly.

'Is that what I was doing?'

'You know you were. I mean it, Mr Falcone, I won't accept anything from you.'

He turned away from her. 'Please yourself. I have an appointment in half an hour,' he said pointedly.

'I'm sorry!' She looked at him nervously. 'You'll be back at eight-thirty?'

'Yes. And as you don't want me to meet your father you'd better come down here.'

'Very well.'

Farrah hesitated about going up to the flat just yet; her father wouldn't be expecting her home for at least another hour and he would obviously wonder why she was home so early. She could hardly tell him that Joel Falcone had brought her. No, that wouldn't do at all.

She walked back in the direction of the town. She had her cheque book with her, and although she had told Joel Falcone that she had a suitable dress, she didn't really. It had been a show of bravado on her part and even though the sort of gown he would expect his companion to wear would make a great hole in her savings she had no intention of letting him see her in anything but the best.

The gowns she looked at were very beautiful, and very expensive, and she tried on several before making her final choice. It had to be something sophisticated, but not too old for her, and the black gown seemed to fit both those requirements. It was what she would call slinky, clinging in all the right places and yet retaining an air of mystery. The thin satin shoulder straps did not allow for a bra, but as she had never had any qualms about the suppleness of her body this didn't concern her too much. The low neckline made the dark curve of her breasts just visible, but the bareness of her throat alleviated the darkness of the dress.

It had just gone five when she entered the flat and her father was just in the middle of making a cup of tea. He smiled at her as she sat down tiredly in an armchair. 'Been shopping?' he indicated the bag in the chair beside her.

'A new dress,' she explained.

'You're going out tonight, then?' he asked interestedly.

'Yes. You're going over to see Uncle Ben, aren't you?'

'Mmm, we'll probably sink a few jars at the local and talk ourselves silly like we usually do.'

'You know you enjoy yourself,' she smiled.

'Farrah, I don't want to seem too inquisitive, but did you talk to Joel Falcone today?'

'He spoke to me,' she corrected. 'I'm sorry, I should have told you earlier.' So much had happened since she left home this morning that she had completely forgotten her father's anguish. 'Joel Falcone has agreed to drop the charges.'

'Oh, that's wonderful!' exclaimed her father. 'At what price?' he asked shrewdly.

Farrah evaded her father's questing look. 'No price, Daddy.'

'No price! But I—— He must have a reason for this, Farrah! Unless you told him about your mother——'

'No!' she denied sharply. 'I didn't tell him anything.'

'Then I don't understand,' he shook his head.

Farrah shrugged, standing up impatiently. 'Perhaps I just caught him in a good mood, Daddy. Everything should be sorted out within the next few days.'

'Did he say anything about my job?'

'No, he didn't! But I should think you'll be sacked, don't you?' she said shrilly. 'It was a silly thing to do and it'll probably ruin the rest of your life.' And mine, she groaned inwardly. 'Mummy wouldn't have wanted you to do it and you know it. I know it was for her, Daddy, but she would hate to know what trouble you've brought upon yourself.'

'Your mother always had second best, Farrah, she didn't deserve to die that way too.'

This was an old argument and one Farrah always lost. She had loved her mother too, and if she had died believing the money for her private nursing came from an insurance policy then perhaps it was all to the good. 'I could have left work and nursed her, Daddy. You know I wanted to.'

'She didn't want that. You're young, Farrah, nursing your mother would have cut you off from your friends, denied you a proper social life. Your mother wanted you to enjoy your youth.'

'And I have, Daddy, but this threat over our heads is worse than any hardship I might have had nursing Mummy. I loved her too, you know!'

Her father put a comforting arm about her shoulders. 'It was better this way, poppet. Your mother died having had all the medical and nursing care there was available. The trip to Switzerland was the most expensive, but I had to make sure the English doctors were right when they said there was no hope.'

'But company money, Daddy!'

'I know,' he said wearily. 'I know it was wrong. I still have a couple of thousand of it, Farrah, I can give that back,' he added almost eagerly.

'A couple of thousand! That won't even dent the twenty-five thousand. He's a powerful man, Daddy, you should have known better than to try and trick him.'

'I wasn't tricking him personally, only the company.'

'He *is* the company.'

'You're a good child, Farrah, but if I had the same odds against me again I would have to act the same way. I'd have to, do you understand?'

Farrah hugged her father tightly, blinking away her tears as she looked at him. 'I understand, Daddy, but it doesn't make things any easier. I still have to work there and people ask me how you are every day. I never know what to say. They all want to know when you'll be well enough to go back to work.'

'I know it's hard for you, Farrah, but you could always leave. You have the experience behind you now, you could easily get a job with another company.'

She shook her head. 'I don't think so, Daddy.' Joel Falcone wouldn't allow it, for one thing. This way he had easy access to her, and also to cause a stir among his own numerous staff. No, the time to change her job would be when all this was over, that would be when she needed her privacy the most. During the next few months she was going to be known as Joel Falcone's new woman, and the reason for the abrupt end of his friendship with Laura Bennett. God, what a mess!

CHAPTER THREE

'HAVING second thoughts?'

Farrah didn't pretend not to know what he meant, grimacing her uncertainty. 'And third and fourth ones too,' she acknowledged. 'But every time the answer comes out the same.'

Her apprehension had started the minute she stepped into his car this evening. His pure sophistication in white suit and black shirt had unsettled her and once again reminded her of his importance. Joel Falcone was a man who had worked himself up from a back-street child to a smooth polished man with an intelligence that baffled many a rival. But this nightclub had made her withdraw even more into her shell of shyness. There were so many celebrities here that she felt completely overwhelmed. And Joel Falcone seemed completely at home among them!

They were seated in a secluded corner, the reddish glow of the room surrounding them in a warm intimacy that was utterly deceiving. Couples were dancing in uninhibited abandon on the floor space provided, and Farrah felt less self-conscious about her revealed curves in the clinging dress after looking at some of the more exotic gowns being worn here.

The service was excellent and unobtrusive—and must surely be costing a small fortune in itself. This certainly wasn't the sort of place she would have chosen to come to, but she realised Joel Falcone must like this sort of atmosphere. He certainly seemed more relaxed, a faint mocking smile never far from those curved sensuous lips.

'Joel! *Darling*!' A tall girl, with long almost waist-length auburn hair, rushed to Joel's side, embracing him effusively as he stood up politely. 'Where have you *been* all evening?' she purred seductively.

Joel Falcone seemed to be withstanding this on-slaught remarkably well, and instead of repulsing this girl's caresses he was actually encouraging her, return-ing the pressure of her lips with equal fervour. 'Mmm,' he sighed huskily. 'You look good, Candida. As to where I've been, I've been sitting here all evening.'

The girl Candida grasped his arm possessively. 'In that case, why haven't you joined the rest of us like you usually do?'

His arm was draped around her waist, his hand rest-ing firmly on her hip. 'I've—um—I've been *otherwise* engaged.' He looked pointedly at Farrah.

Farrah found it difficult to meet the hostile gaze of the other girl, but nevertheless she managed to do so. Glacial blue eyes raked over her, a slight sneer to the girl's heavily painted lips. 'But *darling*——' she began scathingly.

Joel put out a hand and pulled Farrah to her feet, his hold leaving the beautiful Candida and now encircling Farrah's slim waist. 'Farrah, honey, come and meet Candida.'

The two girls looked at each other with dislike and finally it was Candida's gaze that dropped and fell away. Farrah wasn't particularly bothered about the other girl's dislike of her, but she did think that Joel Falcone should have acted less familiarly with her. After all, if she really had loved him and he her then she wouldn't have been able to meekly sit back and wit-ness such behaviour.

'Hello,' Candida said huskily.

'Good evening,' Farrah replied formally.

She felt Joel Falcone's arm tighten painfully on her waist and the smile on his lips for her didn't reach the darkness of his eyes, deep unfathomable eyes that gave away nothing of his thoughts. 'Candida is an old friend, my love,' he chided gently.

So the act had begun! She had to force herself not to cringe away from such a false endearment. 'Really?' she looked at him steadily.

Candida's eyes had narrowed at Joel's protective air and murmured endearment. She pouted at him. 'I thought I was more than a friend, Joel.'

He laughed at her exaggerated air of hurt. 'Don't try to cause trouble, Candy. Farrah doesn't understand your warped sense of humour. And I won't have her hurt.'

The redhead looked away. 'I see,' she said quietly. 'Are you going to join us?'

'I'm not sure.' He looked at Farrah. 'Honey?'

She shied away from such a suggestion, unwilling to meet more of his friends if they resented her as much as the girl did. 'I—I don't——'

Joel didn't wait for the rest of her answer. He shook his head to Candy. 'I don't think so. Not tonight.'

The beautiful redhead gave it one last reckless shot. 'Is Laura coming here tonight?' she asked casually.

She realised her mistake as Joel's eyes became icily cold. 'I wouldn't know,' he said shortly. 'Laura and I no longer discuss our personal social engagements, as you very well know.'

Candida was instantly contrite. 'I'm sorry, Joel, I didn't mean——'

'I know very well what you meant, Candy, and it wasn't anything polite. Now if you'll excuse us I think I'll take Farrah into the other room and do what passes for dancing in this place.'

Farrah followed him wordlessly, pulled along by his hold on her hand. She didn't have time to say goodbye to the other girl, but she didn't think it really mattered, as Joel had said, Candida did not have politeness on her mind. The poor girl had been positively green with jealousy. Farrah shook off all thoughts of the beautiful Candida, at the moment she had something more pressing to think about. She had seen what Joel said they called dancing when they came into the club, and to her it looked more like making love to music!

'Relax,' Joel murmured in her ear, bending down as they danced so that his face was buried in her creamy throat. 'Try to look suitably ecstatic.'

Farrah was much too aware of his hard lithe body pressed close to her own to look anything else but terrified. She had never danced this close to a man before and each muscle and sinew was firmly outlined against her own trembling body. 'How can I?' she asked tautly. 'When you terrify the life out of me.'

Joel moved his head up and away from her. '*I* do, Farrah Halliday? And how do I do that?'

She looked away from him crossly. 'You mock me.'

'I mock everyone, child,' he said with some humour. 'Including myself.'

'But why are you so cynical?'

He shrugged his broad shoulders. 'I have no idea. Unless you count boredom as a reason.'

'Boredom!' Farrah was frankly astounded. 'But you have so much.'

Joel's mouth twisted. 'So everyone keeps telling me.'

Farrah wished they could sit down again, the movement of his body on hers was so blatantly sensual that she felt like part of the man himself. And yet they would have looked strange dancing any other way, everyone seemed to be moving with the same closeness. 'Could we——' she cleared her throat. 'Could we sit down again, please?'

'Sure,' his eyes mocked her silently as he saw her seated before sliding on to the bench seat beside her, his thigh brushing hers. 'You don't like to dance?' He watched her over the rim of his glass.

'Yes, I like to dance,' she said tartly. 'But I wouldn't call that dancing.'

'Just what would you call it?'

'Making love to music?'

She heard him give a deep throaty chuckle and watched as his teeth flashed whitely and his blue eyes crinkled with laughter. 'An apt description,' he toasted her with his glass. 'So you're a prude, Farrah Halliday.'

'I am not! I just think that sort of thing should be done in private.'

'What sort of thing?' He watched the couples dancing for several seconds. 'It's only body contact.'

Farrah wrinkled her nose delicately. 'I didn't like it,' she said firmly.

'Strange, I found it rather—satisfying.'

Farrah knew he had intended embarrassing her, but she blushed anyway. 'Then you're satisfied very easily,' she retorted shortly.

'Oh, but I'm not,' he corrected her softly. 'I'm very difficult to—please.'

She knew this was a double-edged conversation, and she also knew that Joel Falcone was enjoying her discomfiture immensely. 'Tell me, Mr Falcone,' she ignored his dark scowl at her formality, 'why didn't you ask someone like your friend Candida to assist you with your little problem? She's obviously aware of the breakdown of your relationship with Miss Bennett.'

'I should think all my *friends* are,' he said grimly. 'It's been on the cards for some time now.'

'But what—what happened?' Her eyes were like huge green pools of curiosity.

Joel sighed. 'I suppose you have a right to know. Now I may not be the epitome of the perfect male and Laura and I have never been very faithful, each of us having other casual friendships. But I draw the line at having her burst into my apartment just as I was——' he broke off. 'Making love, *you* would call it,' he looked grim. 'With another woman.'

'But you told me that you—that you and she still——'

'Oh, we do, on the odd occasion. Why not? I take Laura as I would take a shower, not a necessity but pleasant on the right occasion. And as for using Candida, I have better sense. I don't intend to gain my freedom from one scheming woman just to get caught in another trap equally disastrous. Believe me, Candida would demand more from me than you do, both physically and in other ways. And I'm not willing to answer to any woman for my actions.'

'I see.'

'Stop looking so disapproving, Farrah,' he chuckled huskily. 'And for God's sake relax! Don't you ever smile?'

'Sometimes. I haven't had much to smile about lately.'

'Look, I'm not going to hurt you. This is all pretence, and it won't last very long.'

'Just long enough for me to be known publicly as your new woman.'

'It may not come to that, Laura and I may be able to settle this privately.'

Farrah looked at him eagerly. 'Could you do that?'

'Maybe,' he said non-committally.

'Oh, Joel, I'd——' she broke off.

He grinned at her. 'Carry on, Farrah, it would be a pity to spoil your effort.'

She looked at him shyly. 'It wasn't such an effort,' she admitted.

Blue eyes narrowed, but he still smiled. 'All the more reason,' he said huskily. 'Just try and forget our reason for being here. I think that our mission has been accomplished. Candy and her friends have been giving us speculative looks for the past hour or more, and since talking to us I should think Candy has told them all who you are. Don't worry, Laura should know within the next day or so that we were seen together.'

'But would it matter to her? You've already admitted that you both occasionally see other people.'

'That's why I told you it would take a couple of months to convince her, my girl-friends don't usually last that long.'

'Tell me, Mr—*Joel*, have you ever been in love?'

'No. It's a luxury that has never been granted me. You've grown very curious, Farrah Halliday. Why the sudden interest?'

Farrah sipped her Martini and lemonade before answering him. 'If I have to spend time with you I may as well make conversation. Most people enjoy talking about themselves.'

'I don't.' He bent forward, effectively cutting off the rest of the room from her vision. 'I would far rather talk about you. Are you as innocent as you look?'

'You've said that once before. I can't help the way I look.'

'Does that mean that the answer is no?'

'No, it doesn't! If by innocent you mean do I sleep around, then the answer is no. So that makes me innocent in your eyes. I've never gone in for casual love *or* lovemaking.'

'Does that mean you're a virgin?'

'It's none of your business! I——'

'Does it?' he repeated sharply.

'I can't—— It—— Oh yes! Yes, it does! Are you satisfied now?'

'No. I'm interested, very interested. Do you have boy-friends, Farrah? Of course you do,' he answered his own question. 'Someone called Nigel wasn't it, and I presume there have been others. And yet none of them have wanted to make love to you.'

Farrah gasped. 'I didn't say that!'

'So they *have* wanted to make love to you. And you've

said no. Why was that, Farrah, are you holding out for marriage? Are you thinking of how privileged that man will feel when you go into your marriage bed pure and untouched?'

There was no mistaking the sneer in his voice and Farrah bridled angrily. 'Like I said, you mock everything.' She shifted away from him and breathed more easily when no longer made quite so much aware of his physical attractiveness. For a few minutes he had held her attention like a magnet, and she was made all too much aware of how easy it was to fall for his charm when he chose to exert it. And she wouldn't give him that satisfaction.

His hand moved to cover her own as it rested on the table, holding her even tighter as her first instinct was to snatch her hand away. 'Careful,' he warned. 'Don't spoil it all now. You've managed very well so far.'

'Thank you very much, sir! How kind you are!'

Her anger made him smile. 'Your eyes are flashing again.'

Farrah blushed. 'Leave my eyes out of it!'

Joel shook his head. 'Impossible. They're really quite beautiful. Are those dark lashes natural?'

'You're prevaricating again.' She was unable to meet his eyes.

'Not me, honey, you're the one doing that. I asked you a perfectly normal——'

'Normal! Nothing about our whole relationship is *normal*! Can we go home now?'

'Yours or mine?' he taunted.

'You to yours, and me to mine,' she said ungrammatically.

Joel picked up her hand, studying the palely painted nails and her slim tapered fingers. 'There ought to be a ring on this hand,' he said thoughtfully. 'A huge emerald to match your eyes. Has no one ever offered?'

'I'll only marry for love. Now can we go home?' she repeated stubbornly.

'It's early,' he replied vaguely, still looking at her hand as it rested in his own much larger one. He looked at his watch. 'It's only eleven o'clock, much too early to leave. I rarely leave before two in the morning.'

Farrah felt a sense of dread. Another three hours with him. In this mood he was far too dangerous for her peace of mind. In a short time they had become much too intimate for Farrah's liking. Joel seemed to be amusing himself with her and he was being deliberately charming. The trouble was her traitorous body was falling for it. Each time he gave her that dark brooding look she trembled with anticipation, of what she wasn't sure.

'If we leave now your friends will naturally assume we're going to your apartment to—to——'

'Make love,' he drawled. 'That seems to be the topic of the evening. And I can quite as well *make love* at two in the morning as I can now.'

Farrah blushed. 'You're embarrassing me,' she shook her head. 'I've never spoken about such things to anyone before, let alone a man I only met for the first time yesterday. Are you always so—so basic?'

He let go of her hand, sitting back to light up a cheroot with his gold initialled lighter. 'No, I enjoy shocking you. Does that surprise you?'

'I suppose not. My naïveté must be very amusing,' she said dejectedly.

Joel was surrounded by thick smoke, his expression unreadable. 'Nothing about you amuses me,' he said harshly. 'On the contrary. It's a long time since I met anyone as fresh and young as you undoubtedly are. It's quite a novelty.'

'There are plenty of girls like me about. We hardly even know the sort of world you live in exists.'

'So you're going to settle for a respectable young man with a semi in the country and the estimated 2·4 children,' he mocked her. 'Or are you going to try and find yourself a rich husband?'

'Neither. All I want is a man I can love with all my heart. You're so cynical, but one day you'll find someone to love. I only hope you recognise the emotion for what it is.'

'I know desire and I know indifference, and that's enough for me. I don't need anything as complicated as love in my life. Now if you're ready to leave?'

'Oh, I'm ready. There's just one thing, Mr—Joel. My father is only forty-five, he has at least another twenty years left to work. I realise you can't give him too good a reference, but if you could just not give him a bad one? He wouldn't do anything like this again, I promise you.'

'I'm not giving him a reference at all——'

'Oh, but——'

'I haven't sacked him, Farrah. He can come back to work any time he likes.'

Farrah looked at him sharply. 'But he—I—— Do you mean it?'

'Sure. Your father made a mistake, a mistake not too many people know about, and I think he's paid for it. But he'll be watched,' he warned her. 'Security advised me to sack him, so they'll be keeping an eye on him. No one else in the company is aware of his—*borrowing*, so he shouldn't find it too difficult to return.'

'You really mean it?' She saw his faint nod, and sighed with relief. 'Oh, Joel, I could *kiss* you!'

'Don't let me stop you.' He watched her below hooded lids.

She blushed and gave him a shy smile, unable to hold back the bubbly laughter she felt in her happiness. 'Oh, Joel, this is marvellous! It's such a relief. Daddy's been so worried. So have I for that matter.'

'I gather the kiss isn't going to be forthcoming? I thought not,' he took in her flushed cheeks. 'That's the first time I've seen you laugh.'

'It's the first time I've really felt happy for weeks.'

Joel looked at his watch again. 'Nearly twelve. I guess we can go now.'

They had to walk past the table at which his friends were seated and it was only polite that he stop to say a few words. Farrah was aware of being thoroughly appraised by men and women alike and it was only Joel's grip on her waist that stopped her running. There were six men and an equal number of women at the table, although none of them actually seemed to be in couples.

'Unsociable tonight, weren't you, Joel?' remarked a tall blond man.

Joel grinned at him. 'Farrah's worth being unsociable for,' he said smoothly.

There was a knowing gleam in the other man's eyes. 'Trust you to come up with someone new and beautiful. Where are you going now?'

'Farrah has a headache,' he explained. He turned to look at her pale face, bending suddenly to kiss her parted lips. Farrah was taken completely by surprise and responded without thinking. She registered firm caressing lips on her own before they were slowly removed. Joel's blue eyes shone down at her in challenge, and to her shame she was the first to look away. He turned back to his friends. 'I'm taking her home now. We'll join you another time.' And with a casual goodbye they left the nightclub.

Farrah was literally shaking. That kiss had got her completely off guard, and she wondered at the need for such a display. Unless Joel was just claiming the kiss she had said she could give him. Whatever his reason had been it had just confirmed his attraction to her and made her all the more wary.

'Calm down, honey,' Joel drawled once they were back in the car. 'You'll worry yourself into an early grave. It wasn't anything important.'

'No,' she said dully. 'I just wish you'd warned me. I could have done something stupid.'

'Instead of which you kissed me back. Simon said you look beautiful, I guess I forgot to tell you that. The dress is perfect, and you have a good figure.'

'You don't need to tell me this. I've been kissed before.'

'I know. That's why I'm not sure why this one shook you so much. It did, didn't it?' he looked sideways at her.

'It was unexpected,' she insisted.

'Why? You surely didn't expect to get away with a bit of hand-holding and a few smiles?'

'You mean there'll be more—kissing?' She hoped her dismay wasn't too evident.

'Quite a lot more, I should say. That was only for starters. My Italian blood calls for something a little more potent than that.'

Farrah moved uncomfortably, wishing to channel the conversation into something less personal to herself. 'Has your family lived in America long?'

'My great-grandfather left Italy as a young child— and was later excommunicated from his religion for a misdeed I won't go into,' he said grimly.

'Your great-grandfather was *excommunicated*! But why?'

'I said I wouldn't go into it.'

'I know, but——'

'Farrah! Stop being so damned inquisitive! If you really must know, he was what was commonly known as a gangster in those days.'

'He belonged to the Mafia!' she cried excitedly. 'I told Daddy——'

'Yes?' he said tautly. 'What did you tell your father?'

Farrah hung her head guiltily. 'I said *you* looked as if you belonged to the Mafia.'

With a screech of brakes the car came to an abrupt halt. 'You said *what*?' Joel demanded between clenched teeth.

'That you looked as if you belonged to the Mafia,' she repeated miserably.

His knuckles turned white as he gripped the steering wheel. 'Don't ever say that again,' he ground out. 'Not even in jest.' He was too angry to be bothered or care about the drivers who were now overtaking them, tooting angrily at his sudden braking.

'That's what Daddy said.'

'Then you should have listened to him. My great-grandfather is dead now, he has been for years, but it ruined my grandfather's life having him for a father. He was frightened of every little shadow, and he trusted no one. That's no way to live.'

'I'm sorry,' Farrah said quietly.

'So you damn well should be. Not every Italian-American is involved in the Mafia, Farrah.' He gave a grim smile, restarting the car. 'You've been watching too much television.'

'I also told Daddy that you couldn't be involved in such a thing because you aren't the violent type, powerful but not violent for violence' sake.'

'Just keep remembering that,' his face was grim.

'Are you very angry?' she asked tentatively.

'Very,' came his uncompromising reply. 'But no doubt I'll get over it.'

'I didn't mean it, you know,' she said nervously.

'Okay, let's forget it,' Joel replied impatiently. 'What does it matter?'

'It obviously matters to you. I didn't realise when I said it that there would be the remotest connec-tion——'

'There isn't! For God's sake, Farrah, just drop the

subject. Let's talk about something more pleasant.
When will you tell your father about his job? I'll be
informing the department of his return tomorrow.
Will he be well enough to return on Monday?'

'I should think so. This news is all that he needs to
cheer him up.'

'Make sure he knows about us before he returns,' Joel
warned. 'The company will be rife with gossip about us
by then, and he could hear it from anyone.'

'Yes,' Farrah said dully. For a moment there she had
forgotten their evening out had been all a pretence.
He had a way of making her forget everything but him
and the sexual magnetism he exuded.

Joel brought the car to a halt outside her block of
flats. 'We'll meet for lunch tomorrow. I'll call for you at
twelve-thirty. Will you be free to leave town tomorrow
evening? I thought we might go to my country house
for the weekend. Can you manage that?'

The whole weekend in his company! 'Is that really
necessary? I thought you said we would leave it a
couple of weeks before—before spending the night together.'

He turned in his seat, his arm resting along the back
of her seat. 'I've changed my mind.'

'What about Miss Bennett? You said she visited
your home unannounced.'

'Not any more she doesn't. I insisted on it after that
incident with her coming in on me like that. I
wouldn't deliberately take you anywhere I knew Laura
was going to be.' He shrugged. 'If we meet by chance
then that can't be helped, anything else would be suspect.'

Farrah looked at him with huge green eyes. 'She's
very beautiful, isn't she?'

'Laura? I guess so, if you find that sort of beauty ap-
pealing.'

'But you did once,' she said daringly.

'I still do, it's her nature that's hard to live with.' He was watching her closely. 'You have green eyes too, but they aren't at all like Laura's. Hers are slanted like a cat's, yours are soft like a kitten. Perhaps that's the difference between you, you haven't found your claws yet.' His mouth twisted. 'But it shouldn't be long now. Once you realise your power over men, I should say.'

'I don't want power over men. I just want someone to love and have them love me.'

'Don't we all?' he said dryly.

'I don't believe it! You said you didn't believe in love.'

His hand moved to the nape of her neck, gently caressing. 'I could just change my mind.'

Farrah withstood his touch with remarkable calm, considering she was trembling inside. 'I doubt it. You're a hardened cynic.'

Joel removed his arm, straightening in his seat. 'You could be right. Will you be okay for the weekend?'

'I should think so,' she admitted reluctantly. 'Although I'll have to tell my father I'm staying with a girl friend. About lunch tomorrow, could I meet you in reception? It's going to be bad enough in the office from now on as it is, without you turning up all the time.'

'Never mind. They'll have the weekend to get over their shock. Some of them might even have forgotten it by Monday.'

Farrah grimaced. 'I doubt it. It isn't the sort of thing you forget easily. I'll go in now.'

His eyes glinted at her in the darkness. 'No goodnight kiss?' he taunted.

'Certainly not! There's no audience now, Mr Falcone.'

'No, I guess not. Oh well, sweet dreams, Farrah Halliday.'

'I doubt it.'

She heard his throaty chuckle as she ran up the stairs to the flat. This might only be pretence, but her first assumption was correct, like the tiger Joel Falcone was dangerous. And he had described her as a mere kitten! She didn't stand a chance against him, she doubted if anyone did.

'Farrah?' her father called when she had let herself into the flat. 'Is that you?'

'Yes, Daddy. Are you in bed?'

'Mmm, I feel extraordinarily tired today, I don't know why,' he lowered his voice as she came to the open door of his bedroom. 'Your new dress is lovely, Farrah. Was all this for Nigel?'

Farrah looked at him with love in her eyes. Her father did look very tired, it was probably all this worry so soon after her mother's death. 'No, it wasn't for Nigel. I—I have something to tell you, Daddy.' She saw him try to repress a yawn and frowned worriedly at his drawn face. 'It doesn't matter, Daddy. It isn't that important, I can tell you tomorrow.'

'Sure?'

She nodded hurriedly, almost eagerly. 'I'm sure. You have a good night's rest and I'll see you in the morning.'

'O.K., love. Goodnight.'

'Goodnight.' She made her way quietly to her own room, undressing slowly in the darkness, her thoughts in a turmoil. She should have told him of her evening out with Joel Falcone and got it over with. This way she was just prolonging the agony. But her father *had* looked tired, much too tired to be worried with any more problems. She only hoped that after hearing of her relationship with Joel he accepted the offer of his job back for what it was, and not as part payment for his daughter. That was the last thing it was!

CHAPTER FOUR

'ARE you completely mad, Farrah?' Fiona demanded for the second time. 'Joel Falcone of all people!' she said in disgust.

The two girls were sharing their coffee break, or rather Fiona had decided to join Farrah by pulling up a chair next to Farrah's desk and sitting down determinedly. Farrah shrugged. 'Why not Joel Falcone?' she asked casually. She was well aware of the notorious reputation she now had. Everywhere she went in the building people were looking at her and gossiping when they thought she wasn't looking. And probably wondering what her attraction was, she shouldn't wonder.

'Because of Laura Bennett!'

'You said it yourself, Fiona, they aren't faithful to each other. They aren't married, you know.'

'Yes, but——'

'Their affair is over, Fiona, it was over long before I came on the scene.'

'Is that what he told you?' Fiona asked knowingly. 'You surely haven't fallen for that old "she doesn't understand me" line?' she said scathingly.

Farrah had to laugh. 'No,' she chuckled, 'he didn't regale me with that one.'

Fiona shook her head. 'Then I don't understand. I didn't think you were the sort of girl to go out with someone of his kind.'

'Forgive my asking, Fiona, and I'm not being nasty, but what does that sort of girl look like?'

Fiona flushed. 'All right, I get your meaning. But he is pretty lethal, and you are going out with him. I wasn't mistaken about Wednesday, was I? You did go up to Mr Falcone's office, didn't you?'

'I did, yes. He's rather handsome, though, isn't he?'
Farrah had known exactly how she was going to act if
anyone began questioning her. It would be no good
declaring her innocence, so she would just have to act
deliberately blasé. It seemed to be working very well,
Fiona was very shocked by her behaviour, and she
wasn't a girl who was easily shocked.

'Fantastic,' she agreed. 'But that isn't the point, is
it?'

'I realise your concern, Fiona, I can even feel grateful for it, but it isn't necessary. Joel's finished with Miss
Bennett,' she deliberately used their employer's first
name.

'Maybe, but does she feel the same way? She isn't
someone to tangle with lightly,' Fiona warned.

Farrah finished her coffee and threw her empty
plastic cup in the waste bin. 'I've never met her,' she
said slowly. 'Although I gather she's a rather formidable lady.'

'I'm not so sure about the lady. But you can't steal
someone else's man and not get an adverse reaction.'

She gave a slight smile. 'I haven't stolen Joel, Fiona,
he wasn't hers to steal.' He would never belong to anyone! 'And Joel does what he wants to do,' she added
truthfully.

'I can imagine,' Fiona said dryly. 'But how did you
meet him?'

Farrah shrugged. 'By accident, in the corridor about
a week ago.'

'Only a week ago!' squeaked Fiona. 'You certainly
became close in a short time.'

'He's that sort of man, you either love him or you
hate him.'

'And you love him?'

No, she hated him! 'I guess so,' she lied.

Fiona stood up. 'In that case there's no point in my

saying any more. You've obviously made up your mind what you want to do. What will you do if Miss Bennett decides to turn nasty and try and get you the sack?'

Farrah paled. It was something she hadn't thought of. 'Joel wouldn't allow that. Anyway, it shouldn't come to that,' she evaded.

'But it may do. He may just be using you to make her jealous.'

'I don't think so, Fiona. He really is finished with her.'

'Oh, well, you know best,' she shrugged. 'Are you joining us for lunch?'

Usually on a Friday all the girls in the office went out to the local restaurant for lunch. Farrah had forgotten all about it. She shook her head regretfully. 'Not today. I have to go out.'

'Meeting Mr Falcone?'

Farrah blushed. 'Yes, I am, as a matter of fact.'

'Well, I suppose you know your own mind.'

As Farrah waited in the reception for Joel Falcone at twelve-thirty she wondered if what Fiona had said was true. How could she know her own mind when she had allowed herself to be browbeaten into this situation? She wasn't usually this weak-minded, and yet Joel Falcone had walked right over her from the start.

She had rung Nigel this morning and cancelled their date for this evening, which he hadn't taken very kindly to. He had liked it even less that she was unable to see him at all over the weekend, finally hanging up the telephone in bad humour.

Joel Falcone stepped unhurriedly out of his private lift, walking over to where she sat with long easy strides. 'Hello, honey,' he pulled her to her feet by holding her hands. 'I didn't keep you waiting, did I?'

'No.' Farrah had to force herself to realise that deep warm smile wasn't really for her, but part of their act.

'Good.' He took her hand, uncaring of the receptionist's gaping face. 'Let's go, then. I've booked a table for twelve forty-five.'

As yesterday the car was waiting for them and it didn't take long for them to drive the short distance to the Italian restaurant Joel had selected. Farrah allowed Joel to choose her meal for her, and relaxed only slightly when the waitress had brought their drinks. They had a corner table and as it was relatively dark in the restaurant Farrah felt very secluded with Joel, and that made her feel nervous. He on the other hand was his usual confident self.

'Had any trouble this morning?' he enquired.

How handsome he looked in his chocolate brown suit and cream shirt! Farrah sipped her drink to steady her nerves. It was quite an experience to enter a restaurant with a man like Joel Falcone, his bearing and harsh good looks instantly commanded attention and the manager of the restaurant himself had seen them to their table.

'Not really. Fiona offered me some advice I can do without.'

'Fiona is the girl you were talking to yesterday, right?' He acknowledged her nod. 'And she told you not to get mixed up with me, especially as I'm your boss.'

'Something like that. I'm glad you find it amusing,' she snapped. 'I had to sit there and take that sort of advice. She thinks I'm a man-stealer.'

Joel laughed. 'I doubt it. Most people know I won't be owned by any woman, and Laura has pushed me just a little too far.'

'I suppose so. But she seemed to think Miss Bennett might get nasty.'

'Undoubtedly she will,' he drew on his cheroot. 'Like I told you, she's a cat when roused.'

'And I'm a kitten.'

'Don't worry, Farrah, I wouldn't let Laura hurt you.'

'You may not be able to stop her. I—er—I have something to ask you,' she said nervously.

She instantly had all his attention. 'That sounds ominous. Has your father been up to something else I ought to know about?'

'No, he has not! But it is about Father,' she admitted. 'Could you—I mean, would you tell him about his job?'

His blue eyes narrowed. 'Why?'

Farrah allowed the waitress to place her meal before her before answering. A delicious aroma invaded her nostrils and she began to feel hungry. Joel had ordered them both chicken, and the sauce covering it smelt absolutely lovely. The rice and peas also looked perfectly cooked, and although she hadn't been looking forward to this lunch out with him she could feel her mouth watering in anticipation of her meal.

'I shall have to tell Daddy this evening about us, but if I also tell him he can come back to work on Monday at the same time he could become suspicious. His pride would never stand it, you know.'

'I guess not.' As she had begun to eat her meal he did likewise. 'Okay,' he nodded, 'I'll see to it this afternoon. Security suspended him, so they can reinstate him. He won't even know I had anything to do with it.'

'Oh, thank you!' her eyes glowed.

'You're easily pleased,' he said softly. 'No kiss offered this time?'

Farrah blushed. 'No! You know I didn't mean it the last time. It's just a figure of speech.' So far today Joel had been the reserved business man of their first meeting, and she wasn't sure if she preferred him like that or in the more provoking mood he was beginning to adopt with her.

'I know that. But it could be interesting nonetheless.'

'Interesting?' she queried. 'I thought a kiss could be many things, but never *interesting*.'

Joel relaxed back in his chair to study her below lowered lids. 'I didn't mean the kiss would be interesting. You're right, a kiss can be many things—affectionate, passionate, repulsive, many things. No, I thought our response to *each other* could prove most interesting. Would you like to kiss me, Farrah Halliday?'

Two wings of colour entered her cheeks. 'I already have,' she pointed out.

'Oh, no,' his face was in shadow. 'I kissed you, *you* didn't kiss me.'

'Then I suppose the answer is no.'

'You only *suppose*? Farrah Halliday, you surprise me. I could just take that as an invitation,' he taunted.

'Well, it wasn't meant as one! I don't even like you.'

'So I gathered,' he replied dryly. 'No one says you have to *like* me. God, what an insipid emotion! I'd rather have desire or just plain hate. But I do not want you to *like* me.'

'I certainly don't *desire* you!' He might have a smooth muscular body and be the most fascinating man she had ever seen, but that didn't mean she had to fall at his feet. And yet a niggling doubt kept entering her mind. Joel *was* fascinating, and she found him very attractive. But she didn't like him!

'If you say so,' he said in a bored voice.

'Don't you believe me?'

'Why should I not? You've never given me any evidence to the contrary.'

'And I'm not going to!'

He sat forward with a smile. 'That's a very definite no, Farrah. I hope I can prove you wrong.'

'You hope—— You hope——?' she gulped. 'What do you mean?'

'Just that I found kissing you quite pleasant.'

Farrah gasped. 'How can you say such things to me!'

'Why not? If we have to spend the next few months in each other's company we might as well take advantage of the situation.'

'You mean *you* might. I can't see any advantage in that sort of situation for me. None at all,' she said firmly.

'I didn't make the suggestion with any advantage to you in mind, you've already had your reward. I could be quite nice to you if you would let me.'

'I can imagine.' She repressed a shiver, of dread or pleasure she wasn't sure.

'I'll bet you can. I don't mean anything physical,' his mouth twisted. 'Young girls and virgins don't need to fear seduction from me. But a mild flirtation wouldn't be a bad idea.'

'A flirtation? With me?'

'Sure, with you. Like I said, it could prove interesting.'

Anger stirred deep within her, deep and volcanic. 'Do you think that just because you'll be denied the company of other women for the next couple of months you can use me to relieve your frustrations! Because let me tell you that I won't be used in that way. I think that was the most hateful suggestion, Joel,' she finished brokenly, all the anger leaving her as quickly as it had come.

'You could be right,' he agreed quietly. 'And I've never yet used a woman just to relieve my frustrations. I may not believe in what *you* call love, but I've never taken a woman just for the sake of it. I'm sure I can manage without a woman for a couple of months,' he added with amusement.

'Then why make such a suggestion?'

'It may relieve some of my boredom.'

'Well, thanks very much! I didn't realise you found me that boring.'

'I haven't—so far. Your flashing green eyes are entertainment enough. I enjoy getting you angry just to see them.'

'You did it on purpose, didn't you!' Farrah said angrily. 'How provoking you are!'

'I know,' he looked at her half-finished meal. 'Have you finished?'

'Yes, thank you. Your teasing robs me of my appetite. It's funny really, the first time I met you I thought you rather frightening, very severe and grim. You still are, I suppose, but you also have a sense of humour, warped, but nevertheless a sense of humour.'

Joel gave a throaty chuckle. 'And I thought you beautiful but very young, and maybe a little shy. I didn't realise you were also very outspoken.'

Farrah looked uncomfortable. 'I'm not usually, but you seem to bring out the worst in me.'

Joel stood up. 'I have noticed,' he returned dryly. 'Wait for me here while I settle the bill.'

Farrah watched him as he chatted idly with the waitress. God, he was so assured and handsome! And she felt proud to be seen with him. But she shouldn't! Her thoughts concerning Joel Falcone were all confused, and her feelings even more so. The thing was, she forgot it was pretence when she was with him, and could feel herself melting under his charm.

She was very quiet on the way back to the Falcone building, unable even to look at Joel Falcone. She had thought only that morning that she hated him; she now knew that wasn't true. And yet she had told Fiona that Joel was a man you either loved or hated. And if she didn't hate him, she didn't love him either.

Joel parked the car, leading her into the building with a firm grip on her arm. 'I'll pick you up about seven,' was his parting comment as they parted at the sixth floor.

Farrah stepped out of the lift feeling faintly disappointed. His behaviour certainly hadn't been loverlike if anyone should have seen them part. But she shouldn't have been feeling disappointed! She didn't like his touch, of course she didn't! But she *had* felt disappointed, that was an inescapable fact.

It was impossible to wipe this out of her mind, and she was still smarting under the knowledge when she got home that evening. The smile she summoned up wasn't one of her better efforts and her father looked at her searchingly. 'Had a bad day?' he asked gently.

Farrah couldn't help but see his air of excitement, and she didn't need two guesses why. 'Not too bad. What's happened to you?'

Her father was bubbling over with the news of his reinstatement and Farrah felt that her efforts on his behalf had all been worth it. It was a long time since she had seen her father this happy, since before her mother became ill in fact, and nothing was going to be allowed to mar that happiness if she could help it. Joel Falcone's demands were cheap at the price. Being nice to him wouldn't be so difficult in the future.

'That's lovely, Daddy, we can go in together on Monday like we used to. I—er—I'm going to Beth's for the weekend, Daddy. I hope that's all right.' Beth was an old school friend and the two of them often visited each other. She had seemed the ideal solution when Joel had suggested they go away together this weekend, and Farrah hoped she would forgive her for involving her in this deceit.

'That's fine, Farrah. It will do you good. I've been quite worried about you since your mother died. You don't have to stay home with me so much. I want you to go out and enjoy yourself like you did yesterday.'

'Yes, Daddy, about yesterday, I——'

'You had something to tell me, I believe. I'm sorry I was so tired when you got home, this business seems to have taken it out of me. I even overslept this morning.'

'I know. I didn't have the heart to wake you.' She couldn't meet the happy glow in his eyes. 'Daddy, last night I went out with Joel Falcone.'

'Joel Fal——? Farrah!' his face was ashen. 'I know you said the dress wasn't for Nigel, but I never dreamt——! Good God, Farrah! Joel Falcone!'

'I know how you feel, Daddy, but I——'

'No, you don't, Farrah!' he interrupted fiercely. 'My daughter has just calmly announced that she's going out with my boss, a man years your senior. You can have no conception how I feel, none at all.'

'But I——'

'Are you seeing him again?'

She bowed her head. 'I already have. We had lunch together today.'

Her father shook his head sadly, the colour starting to flow back into his pale cheeks. 'This is all my fault. You would never have met the man if it weren't for me——' he broke off, his eyes flying to her downbent head. 'That telephone call from security,' he said dazedly. 'Joel Falcone was behind it, wasn't he? You've sold yourself for me,' he finished brokenly.

Farrah stood up. 'I haven't, Daddy, I haven't done that! I met—Joel a week ago, but I didn't tell you. When I went to see him on Wednesday it wasn't our first meeting.' God, she hated lying!

'Had you been out with him before yesterday?' He sat down heavily and Farrah could quite understand what a shock this had been to him. But it was better than going to prison for embezzling, wasn't it?

'No,' she said quietly. 'But I knew we were attracted to each other. I know his reputation, Daddy, but I—I love him.'

'Oh, Farrah! It can only bring you unhappiness.' He looked at her sharply. 'Does he love you?'

'He—he says he does.'

'But you said you've only known each other a week, that isn't long enough for either of you to know how you feel. And it doesn't alter the fact that my return to work is because of your attractiveness to Joel Falcone. No price is too high to pay for something he wants, not even twenty-five thousand pounds,' he said bitterly.

'You're wrong, Daddy. I'm not going to lie to you, of course Joel had the final decision, but Security advised him to give you another chance. And he isn't buying me. We're going to pay him back as much of that money as we can. I'm determined about that.'

'Well, so am I, but it could take years to do.'

She smiled wanly. 'That's what Joel said. But I don't care.'

'Will you be seeing him again, love? I wouldn't dream of interfering in your life, but I can't say I approve of you seeing him. He's too sophisticated, too— too *everything*!'

'I—I should think I will see him again. I *have* to, Daddy, please try to understand.'

'I am trying, love, really I am. Still, this weekend at Beth's will give you time to think, to try and sort yourself out.'

'Yes.' She looked at her wrist-watch. 'I'd better go and pack a few things. I'm leaving at seven.'

'Do you want me to come to the station with you?'

Farrah smiled tensely. 'No, I know Friday is your favourite television night.'

Her father grinned sheepishly. 'I wouldn't mind, love, you know that.'

'I'll be fine, Daddy.' To have her father come down with her was the last thing she needed.

'Shall I get you a snack? You won't have time for much, it's already after six.'

'I'm not hungry. I really couldn't eat a thing.' And she couldn't. This whole thing was sickening to her, and her changing feelings towards Joel Falcone were the worst.

The house was exactly as she had imagined it would be. They had driven down a long gravel driveway to what appeared to be a much larger version of the typical country cottage, with vines and roses growing all over the front of the house. The inside was a vision not to be equalled, with pinewood panels along the spacious walls and thick pile carpets on the floors. Warm golden lights were switched on all over the house, so they were obviously expected.

A tall man in his mid-fifties emerged into the hallway as they entered the house. 'Good evening, sir,' he said very correctly. 'Madam.'

'Miss,' drawled Joel. 'This is Miss Halliday, George. You prepared a room for her?'

George nodded his prematurely snow-white head. 'As instructed, sir.'

'Good.' Joel threw the car keys into the man's hands. 'I left the car in the driveway.'

'Yes, sir. Shall I serve dinner now?'

Joel glanced fleetingly at Farrah. 'Give us ten minutes, George, then wheel it in.'

He led her into a gracious lounge, the only lighting in here from four small lamps placed strategically about the room. A brown leather sofa was placed before a roaring fire and although it was spring it was quite cold, and the fire gave the room a warm intimate glow. A golden carpet fitted from wall to wall with a thick goatskin rug placed before the fire, and restful paintings of the countryside adorned the walls.

'Sit down, honey,' Joel invited smoothly. 'Like something to drink?'

Farrah deliberately sat down in the leather armchair that matched the sofa. 'Just a small sherry, please.'

He raised a mocking eyebrow but poured her the sherry anyway. Tonight he seemed more relaxed than she had ever seen him and was dressed completely informally in white trousers and a snowy white shirt, the cuffs turned back and the buttons open almost down to his waist, with a gold medallion nestling among the dark hairs on his tanned brown chest.

'So,' he handed her the sherry before himself sitting down on the sofa she had shunned, reclining back, legs splayed out as he watched her over the rim of his glass. 'Here we are.'

'Yes,' she answered stiffly. What else could she say?

She had changed into denims and a checked shirt worn below a denim waistcoat as she didn't know how far they would be travelling, and this seemed to be the most comfortable attire. As it turned out they had only been travelling about an hour and a quarter to this house set in the Hampshire countryside, and she wished she had on something more fitting to sit down to dinner with this sophisticated man.

'What do you think of George?' His blue eyes twinkled with amusement.

Farrah was taken aback by the question. 'Well, he's—he seems——'

'Exactly what a correct English butler should be,' Joel mocked. 'Oh, he is. He's been with me fifteen years now. And he manages never to be shocked about anything.'

'Meaning me.'

'Meaning you,' he agreed. 'I've never brought anyone like you here before and yet, George remained completely unruffled. Amazing.'

'Isn't it,' she said tartly.

'Now don't start getting annoyed—and don't deny

that you were, because your eyes are flashing. George is only used to my turning up here. He's probably been wondering for whom he was preparing the room adjoining mine.'

'The room next to yours . . .?' Farrah echoed dully.

'Sure, where else? This has to look convincing.'

A faint knock sounded on the door before George quietly opened it. 'Dinner is served, sir.'

'Thanks, George.' Joel stood up, holding out a hand to Farrah. 'Honey.'

George served them with thick onion soup, steak served with peas and baby new potatoes, and strawberries and fresh cream followed by liqueur coffee. He was attentive and yet unobtrusive, although Farrah wasn't used to such attention when she was eating. She found it slightly embarrassing.

Once they had returned into the lounge Joel dismissed George. 'We won't be needing you again tonight, George,' he smiled. 'That was a delicious meal you prepared us.'

'Yes, lovely,' echoed Farrah, looking at him a little uncertainly.

George bowed. 'Thank you, miss. Goodnight, sir, Miss Halliday.'

'Does George do all the cooking too?' Farrah asked once they were alone.

'Yes,' Joel lit a cheroot. 'He's very adaptable.'

'Would it be all right if I went up to my room now?' she asked hesitantly. George had taken up her small suitcase as soon as they arrived, although she hadn't seen her room yet.

His brows drew together in a frown. 'So early? Aren't you going to entertain me?'

Farrah watched him warily. 'How could I entertain *you*, Mr Falcone?'

'I can think of numerous ways. But we won't go into

them tonight.' He stood up. 'I'll show you to your room.'

The bedroom he showed her into was in beautiful rich gold and white decor, and Farrah loved it from the start. Along one wall was a bedroom unit, a wardrobe either side of a dressing table with a huge mirror and gold trimmings to the wardrobe and drawers. The carpet was pure white and so thick that Farrah longed to sink her bare feet into it, and there was a thick gold continental quilt on the huge double bed.

'It's lovely!' Her eyes glowed.

'I'm glad you like it,' he said sardonically.

Farrah hesitated. 'Does she—does Miss Bennett sleep in this room?'

Joel shook his head. 'No. Laura has never been invited here. This is the one place where I can be private and alone. Why? Would it bother you if she had?'

She threw back her head defiantly. 'Yes, it would. Does that surprise you?'

Joel moved forward, one hand moving up to touch her cheek. 'I guess not,' he said huskily. 'You're a sensitive little thing, aren't you?'

Farrah suffered his touch, her senses stirring against her will as his fingers moved caressingly over her cheek to her parted lips. She held her body rigid and unyielding, although his closeness seemed to be breaking down her feeble barriers. 'Coming from you that sounds like an insult,' she said stiffly, words her only defence.

His dark head bent swiftly and his lips claimed hers in a slow lingering kiss that demanded she respond. Farrah fought for control of her body, and just when she thought she would have to give in he lifted his head, his lips still only inches away from her own. 'Did that seem like an insult too?' His eyes searched her face. 'Because both were meant in the same way.'

She felt mesmerised by those deep blue eyes and

dragged her gaze away with effort. 'Would you mind leaving my bedroom now, Mr Falcone?'

His caressing hands dropped away from her face and he walked to the connecting door she hadn't noticed earlier. 'It was Joel earlier today,' he said mockingly. 'And you didn't answer my question.'

'I've told you before, Mr Falcone, I will not be used. Try your seduction routine on someone else, because I'm not impressed.' Brave words, but not strictly true. If he had persisted with that kiss there was no telling where it would have taken them. Only seconds more and she would have been kissing him back, her arms thrown around his neck in complete abandonment. That kiss was like nothing she had ever known before, and she wished he would go before she made an absolute fool of herself.

'I'm sorry you were insulted, Miss Halliday,' Joel replied coolly. 'But perhaps it was as well.'

She looked at him sharply. 'What do you mean?'

Joel shrugged. 'Only that it would be very unwise of you to become emotionally involved with me. *That* I can do without.'

'Why, you—you—I wouldn't become *emotionally* involved with you if you were the last man on earth. How very conceited you are! I despise you utterly!'

'Good, let's keep it that way. Goodnight, Farrah Halliday.'

Farrah felt like throwing something at the door he closed unhurriedly behind him as he left. How dare he! How could he suggest such an unlikely thing? She sank down on to the bed dejectedly. Was it so unlikely? Wasn't that just what she was doing? Why didn't she admit to herself that Joel Falcone attracted her as no other man had ever done, that she found him fascinating and sensually magnetic? She couldn't admit it because once she had done that his attraction would become stronger!

How could she like him anyway? He was everything she had thought she disliked about a man, very confident, uncaring of women except when it directly concerned him, mocking and completely cynical. And yet each time she saw him she felt more drawn to him.

The door leading off the other side of the room led to a bathroom and she decided to take a shower before going to bed. She didn't feel tired now anyway. As she came back into the bedroom she drew back with a gasp. Joel Falcone lay back on the double bed, his hands at the back of his head as he watched her through narrowed eyes. 'What do you want in here?' she demanded haughtily.

Joel sat up, himself still fully dressed, but enjoying her embarrassment as she held the huge cream bathtowel around her naked body. 'I came to see what you like for your breakfast,' he drawled slowly. 'As you were in the bathroom I waited.'

'Yes, well——' Farrah was very much aware of the limits of the bathtowel. 'Couldn't it have waited until morning?'

'It could, but as I'm here . . .'

'Very well,' she said crossly. 'I have coffee and toast.'

'Fine. So do I. Coffee and toast for two, then.' He walked back to the open connecting door and Farrah had a brief glimpse of green and white decor. 'By the way, Farrah, you have lovely legs.'

'Ooh, you swine! Get out of here!'

He did so with unhurried movements and she could hear his mocking laughter as he moved about in the next bedroom, and wondered how she was ever supposed to sleep with him so near.

CHAPTER FIVE

FARRAH woke to see daylight shining through the window where she had forgotten to pull the curtains the evening before. Some birds were singing happily outside and she wondered what the time could be. Before she had time to sit up and look at her wrist-watch, which was on the side table, Joel Falcone walked into the room, dressed only in a navy blue towelling robe.

He came over to the side of the bed and Farrah could see droplets of water in his hair where he must have just taken a shower. 'Good morning,' he greeted her easily. 'I wondered if you would be awake yet.'

Farrah bridled angrily, all too much aware of how vitally attractive he looked in the short dark robe. 'Well, as you can see, I am. I supposed you're used to walking into women's bedrooms unannounced, but let me assure you, I'm not used to it at all.'

'I've only entered the bedroom, Farrah, not your bed. Does it disturb you, my being here?'

'Of course it disturbs me. I've never had a man in my bedroom before.'

'Then you've never been told how good you look in the morning?' He shook his head. 'Now that's a shame. I've never seen a woman look this good first thing in the morning.'

'And you've seen plenty, I'm sure,' she said sharply.

'A few,' he admitted. 'Enough to know that most of them need a good half an hour and plenty of make-up to make them look anything like presentable.' He smiled at her. 'I trust you slept well?'

'Yes, thanks. What do you want in here, Mr Falcone? Not just a casual conversation, I'm sure.' Farrah was completely unnerved by his attire, or lack of it. She felt sure he was wearing nothing beneath the bathrobe, and the knowledge did nothing for her nervousness.

'True. George should be bringing up the breakfast in a moment, and I think I should be in here with you when he comes in.'

Farrah's face suffused with colour. 'Do you have to? Isn't it enough that he knows we're here together? You surely don't have to look as if you slept with me.'

His eyes taunted her. 'If George looked at you too closely he would know I haven't anyway. No man has ever made love to you, have they, Farrah? My insults to you the first day we met were completely wrong. No man, rich or otherwise, has ever taken you, have they?'

'I already told you that.'

'So you did. It's those unawakened eyes, there's no knowledge of love there at all.'

'Is that a bad thing?'

'Sound insulting again, did I?' He smiled his amusement. 'It wasn't meant to. Although it could prove rather embarrassing if anyone else notices it. My women usually look as though they've been made love to. And you certainly don't.'

'I'm sorry!'

'Don't be, I could soon remedy that.' He made a threatening move towards her.

'Don't you dare!' Farrah backed further up the bed.

Instead of making any further move towards her he gave a throaty chuckle. 'Do you know, Farrah, I don't think anyone else has ever made me laugh as much as you have.'

'I would rather you laughed with me and not *at* me.'

'I'm not really laughing at you, honey, you're too refreshing for that. You intrigue me,' he admitted.

Farrah blushed. 'I don't see why. I'm just ordinary.'

Joel shook his head. 'Never ordinary.' He turned, 'I

can hear George coming up the stairs. Do you want me
to go back to my own room?'

'Yes! No! Oh, what does it matter? My reputation is
in shreds anyway. Daddy thinks I'm something like a
scarlet woman.'

A smile appeared on Joel's lips and unwillingly
Farrah smiled as well, until both of them burst out
laughing. When George entered Farrah's bedroom
after knocking politely it was to find his employer sitting on the side of Miss Halliday's bed and both of
them laughing uproariously.

'Your breakfast, sir, miss,' he said stiffly, leaving the
tray on the side table before leaving the room, his back
rigid with disapproval.

Joel sobered slowly. 'Now we've shocked George,' he
said lightly.

'Oh, dear!' Farrah was genuinely dismayed.

'He'll get over it. Like some coffee?'

'Yes, please.' She felt rather restricted with Joel in
the room. Her nightdress was cotton and perfectly respectable, but neverthless she wasn't going to get out of
bed until Joel left. 'White, one sugar. Does it bother
you that George is shocked?'

Joel brought her some buttered toast and a cup of
coffee. 'Not really. He'll get used to seeing you about.
We'll probably be back here in a couple of weeks' time.
Anyone can see you aren't—you aren't—— Well, what
I mean is, George will obviously blame me. He'll think
I've taken to seducing teenagers.'

'He's supposed to think you're in love with me,' she
pointed out.

'Mmm,' Joel said thoughtfully. 'That's proving more
difficult than I thought.'

'You mean I'm not an easy person to pretend you're
in love with?'

'As I've never been in love, I wouldn't know. But

those trusting green eyes are certainly disconcerting. Some poor man is going to have a terrible battle with himself when he makes love to you—lust over trust.'

'What rubbish!' she retorted, stirred into anger. 'It wouldn't be lust if I wanted it too, it would be a mutual thing.'

'I guess so. But I don't envy him.'

Farrah felt curiously hurt by his words. 'You aren't a very nice person.'

'True. Can you ride a horse, Miss Farrah Halliday?'

'Can I *what*?'

'Forgive me, I thought my English was perfectly clear. Can you, or can you not, ride a horse?' he said precisely.

'That's what I thought you said. And the answer is no. In fact they terrify me.'

'Now that does surprise me.'

'That I don't like horses? I don't see why.' Farrah brushed the breadcrumbs off the bed. 'I was born in a town and have lived there all my life. I hardly ever see a horse, let alone attempt to ride one.'

'That isn't what surprised me. It was the fact that you admitted it.'

Farrah blushed at his intended rebuke. 'It isn't a case of admitting anything. As soon as I'd attempted to get on one you would have known. Do you actually keep horses here?'

'Only two, unfortunately. One is far more spirited than the other, it depends on my mood as to which one I ride.'

'But who looks after them? Not the accomplished George again?'

'The same,' Joel grinned. 'I told you he was adaptable.'

'He needs to be. How on earth does he cope?'

'Very easily. Most of the time he's here on his own,

so he has plenty of time to exercise the horses every day. If you get out of bed now I'll take you down to the stable and introduce you to Sultan and Naomi.'

'I'm quite willing, if you'll just leave the room while I dress.'

Joel's eyes narrowed. 'And supposing I don't want to?'

'Then I won't get up,' she vowed stubbornly.

For answer Joel sat down in the white bedroom chair, arms folded in front of his chest. 'If that's a challenge, honey, I accept.'

'If what's——What do you mean?'

'I try never to refuse a challenge,' he told her. 'Especially from a woman.'

'But I wasn't—I only—— Oh, *please* leave my bedroom!' she begged.

He looked about the room as if seeing it for the first time. 'You're right,' he agreed, 'this *is* your room. It suits you perfectly, gold for your hair and white for your innocence.'

Farrah looked at him uncertainly, not sure if he was mocking her again. He didn't appear to be, although he had the usual cynical twist to his mouth. 'Mr Falcone——'

He stood up, placing his empty coffee cup back on the tray. 'O.K., I'm going. But only because I'm sure your obstinacy would keep you in that bed all day if I didn't back down. You have ten minutes,' he warned.

As soon as he had left the room Farrah jumped out of bed, collecting her bathrobe—just in case he should come back. He seemed to walk into her bedroom as freely as if it were his own. And that curious comment about this bedroom suiting her perfectly. For a moment he had sounded quite poetical. Joel Falcone poetical? Impossible!

She showered hurriedly before donning levis and a

lawn cotton blouse. She had brought some smarter clothes with her, unsure what Joel had meant when he had said country house, but as they were only going to the stables levis seemed the wisest choice. She only had time to apply a coral lip-gloss before her allotted ten minutes were up, and she would be damned if she would be late. She wouldn't refuse a challenge either!

Her bed made and the room tidied she collected up the tray and made her way downstairs before Joel could declare her late. He stood at the bottom of the stairs waiting for her, his black trousers tucked into knee-length leather boots, and his black silk shirt fitting him as if it were tailored on him.

He took the tray firmly out of her hands. 'I didn't bring you here to wait on yourself,' he reproved sternly. 'George could have brought this down.'

'George has enough to do,' Farrah retorted, uncaring of his dark frown. 'I made my bed too,' she added defiantly.

'You'll have George out on strike,' he warned her. 'He doesn't take kindly to interference, thinks it's a slight on his age.'

'But he isn't old!'

'I'll tell him you said so, you'll be a friend for life.' He looked down at the tray with disgust. 'Wait here while I take this through to the kitchen.'

Farrah hummed quietly to herself as she waited, deciding that what this hallway needed was a beautiful vase of flowers on the hall table. Hmm, that would just give it the finishing touch. George was very good at his job, but after all he was a man, and this house lacked a woman's touch.

'I told you,' Joel grinned as he came back, 'he was quite offended.'

'Was he really?' she frowned.

'Well ... Not once I explained, no.' His eyes mocked her.

'Oh you! You're always teasing me,' she said crossly.

'I know. It's a facet of my character I've discovered since meeting you. It's the flashing eyes, of course.'

'You're doing it again,' she warned as he opened the door for her to go outside.

'I can't help it. Perhaps if you wore sunglasses when in my company I wouldn't be tempted.'

'Well, I'm not going to. It isn't sunny at the moment. I would look ridiculous.'

'Oh, well,' Joel shrugged, leading the way around the back of the house and across the garden to the stable. 'You'll just have to put up with the teasing.'

'I just won't let you bait me.'

'Then I would only think up other ways to make you angry,' he said provocatively.

'Oh.'

Joel chuckled as he led her over to a stall where a beautiful black stallion snorted and stamped to tell them he wanted to go out for a run. Joel walked up beside him, talking softly and slowly soothing the horse. 'That's my boy, Sultan. That's my boy,' he crooned, patting the horse lovingly on the neck. 'You're late for your ride today, aren't you, boy? We'll soon put that right.'

Farrah stood back, away from the flaying head of the horse as he tossed and moved restlessly in the stall. He was a beautiful stallion, tall and black and obviously well cared for by his satiny coat. A couple of stalls away stood a smaller chestnut mare, her tiny whinnies calling for some attention to be given to her. Farrah walked over to the other stall, not going up to Naomi but moving nearer to her than she would ever dare to do to Sultan. Naomi was a much smaller horse, with the prettiest, softest brown eyes Farrah had ever seen.

Naomi turned her head as Joel entered her stall, nuzzling into his hand. 'Hello there, beauty,' he smoothed her glistening coat. He looked at Farrah. 'Feel like your first riding lesson?' he quirked an enquiring eyebrow at her.

She backed away. 'N-No. I told you, I'm frightened of horses.'

'Surely not of Naomi? She wouldn't hurt a fly that was irritating her. I'll take Sultan for a ride first and then see about getting you up on Naomi.'

Farrah shook her head. 'I'd rather not. I wouldn't keep it up once we've parted, anyway.'

'You have a couple of months to learn,' he reminded her.

'No,' she said stubbornly.

Joel turned from patting Naomi to look at her. 'You really are frightened, aren't you?'

Farrah turned away. 'Horses are beautiful animals, but they're not for me.'

'Okay,' Joel nodded. 'If that's the way you feel, I'll respect your fear. What are you going to do while I take Sultan out?'

She was surprised at his casual acceptance of her refusal. To a man who appeared to be frightened of nothing her fear must seem a great weakness. 'I—I thought I might look around the garden. Do you have any objection to my picking some of the flowers?'

He shrugged, pulling down a saddle and putting it on the now calm Sultan's back. 'Feel free. Do you like flowers?'

'We don't have any at the flat, but I do like them, yes.'

He swung himself easily on to Sultan's back, and Farrah was struck by the similarity between the two, both were sleek, powerful and beautiful. 'I'll see you at lunch, then. Don't wander off and get yourself lost.'—

'I'm not that much of a towny,' she retorted crossly. 'I do have some sense of direction.'

'I'm glad to hear it,' he grinned at her, urging Sultan out of the stable.

Farrah wrinkled her nose at him and heard him chuckle to himself as he rode off at a gallop. He soon disappeared from view, crouched low over Sultan's smooth neck as they increased in speed, and Farrah wandered slowly back to the house. The front door stood open and as she came in George halted in his progress up the stairs.

He looked at her with polite enquiry. 'Can I get you anything, Miss Halliday?'

'No—No, thank you,' she said breathlessly, rather shyly meeting his eyes. Whatever must he think of her, spending the weekend alone here with his employer? He no doubt thought her behaviour shameless.

'Very well, miss. If you need me for anything I will be upstairs tidying Mr Falcone's bedroom.'

'Thank you,' she said again.

The garden at the front of the house, if it could be called a garden, was more like a riotous jungle of flowers and shrubs. As the house was some way from the road the peace and quiet was somehow unnerving, a silence Farrah wasn't used to, although it became soothing after a while. She walked appreciatively through the sweet-smelling blossoms, careful not to step on any of the smaller flowers as she picked her blooms. The sun was attempting to come out from behind the clouds now and Farrah lay down on the grass, never having felt quite so much at peace in her life before.

She woke to the sound of birds singing and the deep scent of flowers and wondered where she could possibly be. Realisation came quickly, and she scrambled to her feet, a hurried look at her watch telling her it was almost one o'clock. Joel hadn't told her what time lunch was, but she felt sure it must be about now. And she was late! Joel was bound to be annoyed.

She quickly gathered up her armful of flowers—after all, that was her reason for being here—and running through the garden she entered the house, her cheeks flushed and her hair windswept. She called Joel and George, but there didn't seem to be anyone about.

The kitchen was deserted and placing the flowers on a worktop she looked about for a vase. There must be one somewhere in the house. She finally routed one out at the back of the larder and it was almost one-thirty by the time she had arranged the flowers decoratively in its long length, and still no one had returned. It was all very puzzling.

As Farrah entered the hallway, the vase of flowers firmly held between her hands, Joel stormed through the open front door. Stormed was the operative word, his eyes were blazing and he looked positively furious.

'Where the hell have you been?' he demanded savagely, grasping her forearms and knocking the vase out of her hands. It hit the floor with a thud, not breaking on the thick carpet, but spilling its contents everywhere.

'Oh, Joel!' Farrah gasped her dismay, bending down to begin picking up the scattered flowers. She looked up at him reproachfully. 'What did you do that for?'

Joel wrenched her back on to her feet, shaking her ruthlessly. 'I asked you where you'd been!'

'But the flowers——'

'Damn the flowers! Answer me, Farrah, where have you been?'

His mouth was tight with anger and his blue eyes had that icy chill to them that she hadn't seen since their first meeting. She shook her head, dazed by his behaviour. 'I've been out in the garden. I told you I was going there.'

'I know what you told me,' he said between gritted teeth. 'But you weren't there at twelve-thirty when I went to look for you. You've had George and me out looking for you for over an hour now and I walk in and find you calmly arranging flowers!'

'You—— You've been looking for me?' Her eyes were huge and apprehensive, his anger with her a tangible thing.

'Of course we damn well have! George is still out there searching the grounds,' he ran his hand through his already tousled hair. 'Where were you? I called you and when you didn't answer I came to the house. George said he saw you about ten-thirty, but not since then.'

Farrah looked slightly abashed. 'I *was* in the garden, Joel, really I was. I didn't hear you because I—I fell asleep,' she admitted reluctantly.

'You *what*!' Joel looked positively astounded. 'You what!' he repeated loudly. 'No, don't bother to answer that. You fell asleep!' He smote his fist on his forehead.

She was back down on her knees attempting to pick up the flowers. At least down here she didn't have to look at his angry face. 'It was so nice out there,' she mumbled. 'Peaceful, and quite warm in the shelter of the shrubs, and I just—I just fell asleep.'

She finally had to stand up, the flowers all safely gathered back into her arms. There was still the growing wet patch on the floor to deal with, but she would see to that in a moment. For now she had to face Joel, and that was enough to cope with. She looked at him through the multicoloured blooms. 'I'm sorry,' she whispered huskily. 'I didn't realise you would be worried about me.'

'You didn't——! No, I don't suppose you did,' he answered his own exclamation. 'Well, I was. Damn worried!' He pulled her roughly against him, crushing her and the flowers hard against his chest. His arms were like steel bands and his chin felt rough against her forehead. 'Don't ever do that again, Farrah. Not ever!'

'But I——'

She was silenced by the firm pressure of his mouth on hers, and all thoughts of anything but the barricade of feelings she felt at his touch were erased. One of his hands held her head immovable and his lips ravaged hers with anger. Her eyes were closed with emotion and she responded to this kiss that was an attack on the senses. This time there was no thought of denial and her lips opened willingly beneath the brutality of his, allowing him free licence with the moist sweetness of her mouth.

What would have happened next she would never know, a discreet cough behind Joel breaking them apart, and he turned to face George. Farrah was blushing profusely and the flowers were now a sorry sight, crushed beyond recognition. And the front of her blouse was now stained beyond repair.

George entered the house. 'I see you found Miss Halliday, sir.'

Joel still maintained a detaining hand on her arm. 'As you can see, George. Miss Halliday had inadvertently fallen asleep.'

The manservant looked pointedly at the crushed limp flowers. 'In the garden I presume, sir.'

Joel grinned. 'You presume aright. Miss Halliday—accidentally spilt the flowers,' he explained erroneously.

'I did not! You——'

'I helped, I'm afraid,' Joel's grin widened. 'Still, no

harm done. I'll get a cloth from the kitchen and mop up this mess.'

George looked affronted. 'You most certainly will not, sir. That is my job.'

Joel looked at the still indignant Farrah. 'You've upset him, you know, bringing down that tray this morning.'

'And making her bed,' added George.

'Ah yes, don't forget the bed,' drawled his employer, obviously enjoying Farrah's discomfiture.

'I'm sorry. It's just that I'm not used to people doing things for me.' She looked down ruefully at her blouse. 'I think I'd better go and change, I'm slightly wet.'

'Mmm,' Joel blatantly admired the firm outline of her pointed breasts now clearly visible under the clinging material. 'Slightly.' His mouth twisted.

'If you will give me the flowers, Miss Halliday,' George said pointedly, 'I will endeavour to get you some fresh blooms after lunch.'

Farrah couldn't look at either of them, she was so embarrassed. 'Thank you,' she murmured before running up the stairs, her face aflame with emotion.

Once in her bedroom she leant back on the closed door, her breathing ragged. Joel had kissed her. And there had been no witnesses! At least, no intentional ones. George's entrance had been unexpected by both of them. And yet Joel had kissed her, kissed her as no one else had ever done. And she had liked it! She had enjoyed the mastery of his touch and the way his mouth had parted hers. She had been able to smell his after-shave and the not unpleasant smell of perspiration where he had been riding. It was a completely masculine smell and stirred the senses.

She changed into a pink and black flower print skirt and a black vest top tucked in neatly at the waist. Denims were all very well for some occasions, but sometimes she liked to feel feminine, and the fashions were such at the moment that all the skirts were pretty, flowered, and most of all, feminine. She put on wedge sandals that gave her extra height and confidence, feeling she needed plenty of the latter to face Joel again.

Joel had changed too and was now wearing denims and a matching denim shirt. He quirked an eyebrow at her appearance but said nothing. 'Lunch in five minutes,' he said coolly. 'Care for a drink?'

'No, thanks.'

They ate their meal in silence and Farrah was left to wonder what they would do for the rest of the day. Once again they retired to the lounge after their meal and Farrah watched Joel nervously. He seemed different now, more detached—and more like the Joel Falcone she had first known.

'I suppose you're annoyed about that kiss we shared earlier,' he said finally, breaking the silence that was becoming unbearable.

Annoyed! Annoyance was the last emotion she felt! Pleasure, yes, and bewilderment, but never annoyance. She cleared her throat. 'I——'

'It was necessary, you know,' he interrupted.

Her look sharpened. 'Necessary?'

'Mm. I could hear George returning and our conversation wasn't exactly loverlike,' he mocked, his eyes shuttered and unreadable.

Farrah licked her suddenly dry lips. 'I see. So you did it because you heard George.'

'What else?' He quirked an enquiring eyebrow.

'Quite,' she managed a tight smile. 'I did wonder. It was rather sudden and you took me by surprise.'

'Is that your excuse for responding?' he asked cruelly.

Farrah's eyes flared. 'I——'

'Don't deny it, Farrah, I know response when I feel it. And you were definitely responding!'

'Okay, I admit you know how to kiss. But then you've had plenty of experience,' she added bitchily.

Joel laughed throatily. 'If you're trying to annoy me, Farrah, you're going about it the wrong way. Now pull another stunt like your disappearing act this morning and I *might* lose my temper.'

'It was *not* a stunt! I genuinely fell asleep.'

'Oh, I believe you. Your eyes were all drowsy as if from lovemaking, and as I'm sure it wasn't that it had to have been from sleep.' He stood up. 'I'm going into town. Do you want to come?'

'I—no—no, I don't think so,' she said stubbornly.

Joel shrugged. 'Please yourself.'

'I intend to.'

'That's what I thought.'

Farrah regretted her stubbornness later in the afternoon. She really didn't know what to do with herself. She could have offered to help George, but she had probably offended him enough for one day. The garden bore another hour's perusal, and she went into the stable and spoke to Naomi for a while but in the end felt slightly ridiculous talking to a horse. All this beauty was very enjoyable, but not alone. It was the sort of atmosphere that needed to be shared with someone.

Joel finally arrived home about an hour before dinner, handing her a gaily wrapped parcel before pouring himself out a whisky at her refusal. 'Aren't you going to open it?' He indicated the parcel in her lap.

She picked it up, staring at it fixedly. 'I—— You didn't have to buy me a present.'

'I know that. I thought you'd like it.'

'What is it?'

He took a gulp of whisky. 'Open it and see.'

Farrah slowly stripped off the paper, revealing an expensive-looking flat jewellery case. Her fingers trembled as she slipped the catch to open the box, almost dropping it as she saw what it contained. Nestling among a black velvet lining was a platinum bracelet, emeralds set between the links and diamonds surrounding the emeralds. Farrah had never seen anything so beautiful.

She looked up to encounter blue eyes studying her intently. 'Is it real?' she whispered, shaking her head at her stupidity. 'Forget that question,' she smiled shakily. 'Of course it's real.' She took it out of the box, loving the shine and glitter of the jewels.

'There's a ring that goes with it, but I'm having it made smaller.'

'A ring?' Her eyes searched his face avidly. 'What sort of ring?' Suddenly she felt breathless, and she waited anxiously for his answer.

Joel shrugged. 'Just a ring. It will match your eyes,' he gave a half smile. 'Maybe it won't flash quite as much, but it is the right colour.'

'But—but why?'

'You said you wouldn't accept any money from me. The jewellery I give you can be sold when all this is over. This way your pride doesn't get hurt.'

Farrah snapped the lid of the jewellery case shut. 'I see,' she said tightly. 'Thank you for thinking of my pride.' Her smile was bitter. She had every intention of returning anything he gave her, anything at all. 'I'm not really hungry. I think I'll go to bed now, if you don't mind. Thank you for—for the bracelet.'

He nodded his head in dismissal. 'Goodnight, Farrah. If you change your mind about dinner just ask George for a tray. By the way, we'll be returning to town in the morning.'

Farrah rushed out of the room, once in her bedroom dropping the jewellery box on the dressing table. What a hateful, hateful man he was! How dared he insult her by offering her jewellery in this way! How could he be so cruel? Tears coursed down her cheeks and she sobbed uncontrollably. She hated him!

No sooner did it seem she had fallen asleep than she was woken up again. Something was wrong, very wrong; it only took her a couple of seconds to realise what. She could hear raised voices from somewhere in the house.

She sat up in bed as Joel quietly entered her bedroom. 'What's going on?' she demanded.

He seemed quite unperturbed by the noisy shouting, putting his hand over her mouth to silence her. 'Now listen to me, Farrah, this isn't the time for hysterics.'

Farrah removed his hand. 'What's happening?'

His teeth gleamed whitely in the darkness. 'Laura is downstairs, obviously hoping to catch us here together, and believe me, she's going to make quite a scene.'

CHAPTER SIX

'SHE's *what*!' squeaked Farrah, her eyes going worriedly to the closed door.

'You heard me.' His body came nearer to the side of the bed and she realised he was dressed only in pyjama trousers, his brown torso bare in the glow of the moon. Her first instinct was to move away, but Joel stilled her nervous movements.

'H-How do you know she's here?'

Joel chuckled. 'Luckily enough I heard her arrive a few minutes ago. Poor old George is downstairs at the moment trying to stop her coming up here and discovering us. That will only make her all the more determined.'

'Do you have to sound so pleased about it?' Really! The man was impossible. He invaded her bedroom, his mistress was downstairs, and he found it all amusing!

'Why not?' His eyes gleamed devilishly in the darkness. 'This is what we wanted, isn't it? The sooner it starts the quicker it will be over. Now,' he said more seriously, 'I'm going downstairs, I want you to stay up here out of the way—you aren't the best actress in the world where I'm concerned. And the less Laura knows about you the better. I should think she'll be a real bitch, but don't worry, I can handle it.'

'Now that makes me feel a whole lot better,' she said sarcastically.

'It should. Laura can be quite formidable when she chooses, it's all that acting experience. Now,' he turned, 'just stay here like I've told you to,' he gently touched her cheek. 'This shouldn't take too long. I didn't want it this way, honey, I would have preferred to end things amicably, but she wouldn't accept that. You have no need to feel guilty about anything.'

'I know that,' she snapped. 'You forced me into this charade. And I've hated every minute of it!'

'Every minute?' he taunted.

'Every single one!' she said vehemently.

With a mocking smile in her direction he quietly left the room. Farrah stared up at the ceiling sightlessly. What a situation to have found herself in, involved with a man like Joel Falcone.

God, why should she lie here like a zombie! Joel Falcone could be saying anything down there, be involving her in all sorts of intrigues. She had a right to know what was going on, a right to know what was being said. It didn't take her long to put on her wrap and let herself quietly out of the room. She crept stealthily down the stairs, fearing Joel's anger if he should see her.

Only having seen her on the screen before, Farrah had to admit that Laura Bennett was the most beautiful woman she had ever seen. Long black hair cascaded over her shoulders and far down her back, and she had green slanting eyes, a small nose, and perfectly painted lips. She was very petite, and Farrah felt sure that if she stood next to her she would feel monstrously large. As it was, all she could do was stand behind a perfectly composed Joel, held immobile by their conversation.

'Laura,' he said smoothly, as if he were quite used to these scenes in the early hours of the morning. 'This is a surprise.'

Farrah instantly revised her opinion of Laura Bennett being a beautiful woman as her top lip sneered back and her eyes hardened to green pebbles. 'Not a pleasant one, I'm sure,' she mocked, moving further into the light.

Joel regarded her mockingly. 'May I ask why you've honoured me with this visit?'

Laura Bennett spotted Farrah as she stood dazed by Joel's calm attitude. If she had come here and found her boy-friend apparently spending the weekend with another woman she would have wanted to scratch her eyes out. Laura Bennett looked as if she felt the same way. 'Candy was full of some new girl you had in tow, and as I'd tried yesterday and today to reach you at your apartment I guessed you must be here. As you have this silly idea of not installing a telephone to protect your privacy I had to drive down here. I didn't expect you to actually have *her* here.' Her eyes glittered her dislike at Farrah.

Joel looked at her darkly as he realised her presence. '*Her* name's Farrah.'

'So I gathered from Candy.' She looked at Farrah critically. 'Surely she isn't woman enough for you, Joel. I always thought your tastes ran to something more— sophisticated.'

'So did I.' He gave that chilling smile that Farrah knew meant trouble. 'But Farrah's something different.'

Green eyes narrowed to slits. '*How* different?'

'Just different. Now would you mind leaving?'

'But, Joel, I came here to——'

'I'm well aware of what you came here to do, Laura, and this time it won't work. Farrah is staying here with me, you are not.'

'Do you mean this, Joel? Does *she* mean more to you than I do?'

'A straight answer?' His eyes were as chilly as hers were stormy. 'Then the answer is, yes.' He shrugged. 'I tried to tell you, but you didn't want to listen.'

Laura Bennett suddenly didn't look so sure of herself. 'You don't mean this, Joel. You're not actually serious about her?'

He shrugged. 'Why not? She's beautiful and I want her, it's as simple as that.'

If only he meant that! Farrah's heart had skipped a beat at these words, and she realised just how much she was attracted to him. She was falling in love with the man! Oh, God, no!

'You'll never get him, you know,' Laura spat the words at Farrah. ·

Joel interceded before she could make any reply. 'I shouldn't be too sure of that. I love her,' he announced calmly.

Farrah recoiled from the open venom in those slanting green eyes, and the anger in that tightened red mouth. 'Do you mean to tell me you're seriously considering marrying this girl?'

He nodded. 'That's exactly what I mean.'

'Well, I won't stand for it, Joel!' She marched purposefully to the front door. 'I'll leave you with your little—girl-friend for now, and wait for you to come to your senses. I give her three weeks at the most,' she sneered, 'and *then* we'll see how you feel about her.'

The door slammed behind her, leaving Farrah looking slightly bemused. 'I—you—she——' she stammered her confusion.

Joel turned to her, his eyes darkening at the distress clearly written in her face. He pulled her into his arms, crushing her hard against him. 'Don't look like that!' he moaned into her throat. 'No one is going to hurt you, least of all Laura.'

Farrah was only aware of Joel, of his tense body curved intimately into her own. 'I—— Please, Joel,' she murmured huskily. 'Let me go.'

'I will.' His lips were doing strange things to her neck and shoulders, nudging impatiently at the thin shoulder-straps of her nightgown. His hands weren't idle either, moulding her body against his and making her fully responsive to his arousal. 'In a moment,' he muttered tautly.

Farrah was crushed hard against him as his mouth

came down forcefully on hers, and it was pleasure and pain mixed up together. Joel knew exactly the right things to do to make her forgetful of their surroundings and the real circumstances of this unexpected occurrence, and soon her arms were about his shoulders and her hands entwined in the thick vibrant hair that grew low down his nape. His muscles rippled beneath her touch, and she caressed his back lovingly.

'Joel! Oh, Joel!' she groaned deep within her throat, loving the way his hands moved over her body, gently and yet with a mastery that took her over completely, body and soul.

His lips took possession of hers yet again, arousing her until her body moved impatiently against his, urging for his full possession of her feverish senses. 'Wait, child. Wait!' he urged shortly, devouring the soft skin of one revealed breast.

His words brought her to her senses in a way nothing else could have done, and she began pushing at him to stop these caresses that were destroying her and any self-respect she might have had. God! His mistress had just left the house muttering threats against both of them and she was allowing him to make love to her like a wanton! She was disgusted with herself, absolutely disgusted.

Joel looked at her through glazed eyes and made a move to pull her back into his arms. His face darkened as she fought him with all her strength. Sighing, he stepped back, his eyes still full of sleepy passion. 'What's wrong now?' he grated.

She watched the firm play of muscles as he moved, drawn to him still in spite of herself. She loved this man! She *loved* him! She pushed him further away, turning her back on him to run a confused hand through her short tousled hair. This just couldn't be happening! She turned to face him again and found him as composed and cynical as usual.

He gave a mocking smile. 'If you're trying to cool the situation down, honey, I should go put a little more on. In that get-up I can see all of your beautiful body clearly outlined. Pure perfection,' he mocked.

'Oh, you!' She hurriedly turned away again, conscious of his eyes still on her as she moved, her cheeks blazing with colour. 'Are you going to stand there all night?' she snapped at him, unnerved by his naked chest and smouldering eyes.

He laughed huskily. 'I could come to your room—but I won't,' he added tauntingly. He moved past her and began ascending the stairs, only to stop again as he heard someone knocking on the door. It sounded again as he turned to listen.

Farrah looked at him sharply. 'Miss Bennett?'

He grinned at her. 'I doubt it, Laura wouldn't be that polite. At a guess I would say it's George. Come in, George,' he called loudly.

She heaved a sigh of relief as the manservant came in from the kitchen, dressed incongruously in a checked dressing-gown and chocolate brown pyjamas. She had to repress a smile and she saw Joel had trouble hiding his amusement.

'I'm sorry about that, sir,' George said stiffly. 'I did try to stop Miss Bennett, but——'

'It's okay, George, I understand.' Joel smiled, his silk pyjamas trousers resting low down on his hips. 'Trying to stop Laura is like trying to stop a bulldozer.'

'Yes, sir.'

Joel grinned at his discomfiture. 'Okay, George, let's get to bed now and all try and get a good night's sleep. We'll be leaving you to your peace and quiet tomorrow. Miss Halliday and I will be leaving shortly after breakfast.'

To try and sleep was much more difficult than it sounded, and it was a hollowed-eyed Farrah who came

downstairs the next morning. Her toast lay untouched
on the tray, but she had emptied the coffee-pot.

George took the tray from her as she reached the bottom of the stairs. 'Mr Falcone is in the lounge, Miss
Halliday.'

She managed a wan smile. 'Thank you, George. And
thank you for looking after me so well. I loved the
flowers in my room.' George had gone one better yesterday, putting flowers in her bedroom as well as the hallway.

Joel gave her a cursory glance as she quietly entered
the lounge, slowly putting down the newspaper he had
been reading. The navy sweat-shirt and denims he wore
were as casual as her own attire, he was obviously ready
to leave. His eyes narrowed as he looked at her. 'You
slept badly.' It was a statement, not a question.

'What did you expect!' Farrah exploded, all the
pent-up emotion of the last few days coming to the fore.
'You may not be bothered by the situation we found
ourselves in last night, but I am. You were so calm,
weren't you, quite unnerved by Miss Bennett's unexpected arrival. Well, I found it degrading and disgusting! I felt like someone you'd picked up casually for
the evening and decided to sleep with.'

'Calm down, Farrah. Laura——'

'Calm down! *Calm down!* How can I calm down?'
Her hands wrung together nervously. 'It was all so
humiliating. And you *enjoyed* it!' she accused.

'Sure I did. Laura gave a wonderful performance.
An audience would have loved every minute of it.'

'An audience? What are you talking about?'

He shrugged his shoulders. 'Just that Laura loves to
act the wronged woman. And usually she gets away with
it—because I let her. Last night must have come as a
nasty shock to her. Whenever she hears I'm interested
in another woman she comes to my apartment and—

well, I'm sure you can use your imagination. But last night it was different, *you* were already in my bed, so she didn't have the chance to do her usual scene. I must say, it was quite a change.'

'You mean she came here to——? And when she saw I——? Oh, God!' Farrah slumped down into a chair, her face even paler. 'This is terrible!'

'I don't agree, I think everything is working perfectly.'

'Of course it isn't! You heard her, she has no intention of quietly slipping out of your life.'

'She will—in time. Give our relationship three weeks, she said. Well, we'll still be together then and for as long as it takes. Her pride won't allow for her to be humiliated for long. I would prefer that the breaking up of our business and personal relationship isn't known by too many people, and I think it's publicity Laura can do without.'

'Then I won't be in your life for long?'

'Probably not.'

'You really think so?'

'I've said so, haven't I!' he snapped. 'Now let's leave if you're ready.'

Farrah thought it wise not to say any more, sitting quietly in the car as George called Joel back to the house for something. There was a black scowl on his face as he got back in beside her and Farrah was shortly to know why.

'Here.' He threw something into her lap before starting the engine and putting his foot down hard on the accelerator. 'George thought you might have forgotten it,' he said harshly. 'But we know better, don't we?'

She looked down aghast at the jewellery case containing the emerald and diamond bracelet. She had left it on the dressing table where she had dropped it the evening before, expecting George to find it after they had left and return it to Joel at a later date. Instead, she had been found out, and Joel was obviously furious about it.

'Thank you,' she mumbled quietly.

'Is that all you can say? You did it on purpose, we both know that.'

'I don't want anything from you.'

'So you keep telling me. Then how are you to receive payment? I thought all women liked jewellery. I've never had one refuse it before. You don't even have to sell it if you don't want to. Keep it, it'll grow in value— something for your old age. But *don't* try to make me feel guilty about using you, because it won't work.'

'I know that,' she said bitterly.

'Your opinion of me isn't very high, is it?' he asked tautly.

Farrah kept her eyes averted, knowing that to look at him would be her undoing. She loved him, how could her opinion of him not be high! 'Did you ever doubt it?' Her words were stiff and stilted.

'I guess not,' he replied wearily.

After all that had happened to her over the weekend she was surprised that she could go to work so calmly on Monday morning. She and Joel had parted very badly the morning before, and if she were really his girlfriend she would have doubted that she would ever see him again. But as the situation stood between them she knew Joel would be in touch during the next couple of days. Nigel had rung her the evening before and reluctantly she had agreed to meet him for coffee this evening in a back-street café they frequented.

Angie called her into her office later that day and Farrah wondered what she had done wrong. Angie was a busy woman, with a tight schedule, and she didn't waste time lightly. A woman in her mid-forties, she managed to look much younger, her blonde wavy hair perfectly styled and her face beautifully made up. Farrah had always found her a friendly easy-going boss, but she didn't look too happy at the moment.

Her office was sectioned off from the main department and Farrah shut the door behind her at Angie's request. 'Sit down, Farrah,' she said in her soothing well-modulated voice, waiting until Farrah had complied before continuing. 'I'm sure you can guess what I want to talk to you about.'

Farrah blushed, beginning to look uncomfortable. She had thought Anglie wanted to talk to her about her work, but her opening words implied otherwise. 'I think so,' came her husky reply.

'I don't usually interfere in the private lives of my girls, what you do out of work is your own affair. But this time it's different, your private life is overlapping your working one. I didn't believe it at first, but as Mr Falcone never comes down here but prefers me to go to his office, I can only believe that your working here prompted his appearance in the department.'

'He said he had to see you about something,' Farrah mumbled miserably.

Angie smiled. 'Oh, he did, but like I said, I usually go to him. The girls are completely in awe of the whole thing, and I must say I'm a little astonished myself. The bosses have never made any secret of the fact that they have one of these "modern" relationships, sexual freedom and all that, but I have never before known his attention to linger on one of his employees. What I'm really trying to say, Farrah, is that Mr Falcone isn't the constant type, and things could be pretty awkward for you here when your—relationship is over.'

'I realise that. If it gets too bad I'll just have to leave.' Farrah had already faced the fact that this was a strong possibility, but perhaps she needed the change anyway. With this experience of working on a magazine behind her, she would probably be able to get a junior reporter job, something she had always wanted to do.

'Your father works here too, Farrah, it isn't only you who's involved. I always thought you were one of my more sensible girls, but this business with Mr Falcone is completely out of character.' A puzzled frown marred Angie's creamy brow.

At last someone had realised that! Farrah definitely wasn't the sort of girl to have a promiscuous affair, even if she loved the man involved as she did Joel. The pain and agony of parting wouldn't be compensated for in the brief time the affair lasted. 'You can't dictate these things,' she said slowly. 'It just happened.'

'But you must admit it does make things awkward?' Angie watched her nod of confirmation. 'If I put your name forward now for transfer everyone will assume it's because of your relationship with Joel, which it wouldn't be. I have never considered personal relationships when dealing with my work and the people I work with.'

'Does that mean ...?'

'That I was considering transferring you?' Angie finished for her. 'I wasn't just considering it, Farrah, it was a certainty.'

'Was?' she echoed, with a feeling of dread.

Angie nodded. 'I'm afraid so. I hadn't forgotten that's what you wanted to do, and patience often brings its own rewards. I had in actual fact already made tentative enquiries about getting you transferred to one of the newspaper sections. This business with Mr Falcone has put paid to that, I'm afraid. Everyone may consider it a bonus to have you in their section at the moment, but once the affair cools it will be a different proposition. You understand what I'm saying, don't you?'

'That my involvement with Joel has ruined my career,' Farrah said dully.

'I'm afraid for the moment it has, yes.'

'I see.'

'I just don't understand you, Farrah. Granted, Joel Falcone is a good-looking devil, but then devil just about fits him. He's a hard, ruthless man.'

'I know.'

'And yet it makes no difference?' Angie asked sympathetically.

'None at all.' How could it, when she had no say in the matter.

Angie sighed. 'Oh well, I tried. I feel slightly responsible for you with the recent loss of your mother, but I can't live your life for you. You have to make your own decisions and consequently take responsibility for your own mistakes.'

'I'm sorry you feel I've let you down.' Farrah felt quite guilty now, about something that wasn't her fault. Joel had warned her this wasn't going to be pleasant, and now she was beginning to see just how *un*pleasant it could be. Already she had had a face-to-face encounter with his mistress, and now it was starting to affect her day-to-day living, namely her work.

'I think you've let yourself down, Farrah, not me. But as I've said, you have to make your own decisions, and at the moment you feel you're making the right one. I've had my say, I won't mention it again. Unless it affects the department,' Angie added darkly.

Farrah was conscious of the other girls in the office looking at her as she walked back to her desk, all of them probably wondering what had taken place in the office just now. Well, she wasn't going to tell them.

Her father was much more his jovial self that evening, talking animatedly about the day's happenings. She could at least feel happy for him, even if her own day hadn't turned out so good. Joel hadn't called her at all and in a way she felt relieved. If he had wanted to meet her this evening she would have had to refuse him, and she didn't think he would appreciate her wanting to meet Nigel. Oh, damn the man! He had already upset her career, why should she allow him to interfere in her social life too?

Things had been progressing very nicely with Nigel until the advent of Joel Falcone into her life. But she had no doubt that if this thing did become public, Nigel wouldn't be waiting for her at the end of it. Why should he? He too had a career to think about, and he too worked for the Falcone organisation.

The two of them had met in the canteen one day, when Nigel had come over from one of the Falcone newspaper sections to discuss an article with Joel that he was working on. His over-long hair and casual, almost scruffy appearance had marked him as a man who wouldn't conform. At twenty-six, seven years Farrah's senior, Nigel had grown up in an age where long hair was normal, and he saw no reason to change his appearance to suit other people. Fortunately he was good at his job, and it was recognised that occasionally his appearance helped him get a story that otherwise might never have come to light.

Despite his appearance Nigel had instantly made a hit with her mother and father, and he had been of great strength to her during the last weeks of her mother's illness. They had been dating casually for three months now, and during the last few weeks Farrah had started to think it might develop into something more serious, but not now. She had learnt during the last few days that for her love wouldn't grow gradually, but had come suddenly and swiftly—and with completely the wrong man.

Nigel called for her at eight-thirty, and she couldn't miss the look of relieved pleasure that passed over her father's face. Poor Daddy, he was so concerned over this friendship with Joel Falcone. If he only knew, it was all for him!

'What happened to you over the weekend?' Nigel sat

down opposite her in the café where a lot of their friends gathered, pushing over her preferred strawberry milk-shake to his coffee.

'I went to see Beth.' She evaded his eyes. Nigel wasn't stupid, and working at the Falcone organisation he was bound to hear rumours sooner or later. Her poor father had been plagued with guarded but obvious questions all day, and he hadn't taken kindly to it. A lot of people knew she and Nigel had been dating the last few months, and she felt sure he would soon have his fair share of questions from curious people.

'Enjoy yourself?' He watched her over the rim of his cup. His eyes were blue, like Joel's, and yet that was where the similarity ended. Nigel's were a lighter blue and what she called smiling eyes, and Joel's were deep fathoms she could almost drown in, enigmatic eyes that gave nothing away, and weren't intended to. Joel was an altogether enigmatic man, and it was through choice.

'Yes, thank you,' she replied stiltedly.

'And where did you go on Thursday? It's almost a week since I saw you.'

'I—er—I——'

'You had another date, huh?' Nigel watched her closely.

'Would you mind if I had?' Farrah rested her elbows on the table, watching his reaction to her question closely. He didn't appear to be annoyed, but she knew he could be as straight-faced as Joel when he chose.

'Jealous, you mean?' Nigel relaxed back on the bench seat of their booth, his checked shirt unbuttoned and tucked carelessly into his faded denims. 'I could be, but I don't know if I have the right. We've never agreed not to date other people.'

'No—no, we haven't.' She licked her lips nervously. 'You're right, I did have a date with someone else.' Her milk-shake remained untouched in front of her.

'Anyone I know?'

Anyone he knew! She could have laughed at the irony of the question. Of course he knew his own employer! She shook her head. 'I—I doubt it,' she lied.

Nigel pursed his lips. 'I see. Did you have a nice time?'

Farrah laughed nervously. 'You're very serious tonight, Nigel.'

He shrugged. 'I'm interested, that's all.'

'In that case, yes, it was quite nice.'

'Did you go anywhere new?'

'Just a nightclub, nice for a change, but not really that exciting.' The nightclub hadn't been exciting, but the man with her certainly had been. Any other man paled into insignificance when compared to Joel, and much as she liked Nigel he could only ever be a friend to her now—if he would let her be once he found out about herself and Joel Falcone.

'You aren't going to tell me, are you?' His cup clattered back into the saucer, and he looked at her accusingly, his blue eyes blazing his anger.

Her eyes widened at his sudden anger. 'T-tell you what?'

'Oh, come on, Farrah, I gave you every chance to tell me. I asked you leading questions, and then I asked you outright, and still you don't tell me. I know who you were out with on Thursday. I know, Farrah!'

'Then why ask me?' Her eyes sparkled.

'Because I wanted you to tell me yourself, to tell me it wasn't true, that there'd been some sort of mistake! There've been plenty of people to tell me of your affair with Joel Falcone, plenty of well-meaning vindictive people who thought I should know.'

'Then you've known all the time! Why didn't you just say so instead of tormenting me like this? Yes, I saw

Joel on Thursday! And I'm not ashamed of it!' And miraculously she wasn't any more. She loved Joel, and it wasn't an emotion she would hide and feel guilty about any longer—except to the man himself. She could never betray her feelings to Joel, he wouldn't want her love, it was an emotion he didn't recognise. He said he knew desire and indifference, and he wasn't indifferent to her, he couldn't be after that incident yesterday morning.

The other kisses he could blame on proof of their affair, but they had been alone in the hallway, and his desire had been all too evident. Surely that was a start, something for her to cling to. And at the moment she needed something very badly. She felt as if she were slowly going under, with no way out of the situation but pain and misery. Perhaps she was, but once Joel had his emotional and financial freedom from Laura Bennett he would drop *her* too. She had to make the most of this short time spent in his company.

Nigel looked defeated. 'So this affair with him is serious?'

'Yes,' she agreed huskily.

'Then I may as well drop out of the picture. Once you have someone like Joel Falcone in your system it's a hell of a job to get them out, and I don't think I'm the man to do it. You like me, but you *love* him.'

'I'm sorry, Nigel, really sorry. And I'm also sorry you had to find out this way.'

'It's all right, Farrah, you don't owe me anything.' He stood up. 'I think I should take you home now. Don't you?'

She nodded. 'Yes.' There was nothing else she could say.

CHAPTER SEVEN

'WHERE were you last night?' Joel asked coldly. 'I tele-phoned you about nine o'clock and your father said you were out. I got a very cool reception from him alto-gether.'

'What did you expect?' Farrah snapped. 'My father dislikes this supposed relationship intensely, and makes no secret of the fact.'

'I gathered that,' Joel said dryly.

He had called her at the office today and the two of them were now sitting in a nightclub similar to the one they had visited on Thursday, and with Joel equally well known by the other patrons. Farrah was wearing a long cotton flower print skirt, complemented by a cream cotton lace top in a gypsy style and finishing shortly at the waist. Joel's eyes had darkened apprecia-tively when they had met, but the look was quickly masked.

'Can you blame him?' she asked tautly. 'You can't expect him to welcome you with open arms.'

'I don't expect him to hate me either.' He was his usual relaxed and cynical self, having made no mention of their stilted parting on Sunday morning, and she was reluctant to do so. What did it matter anyway, nothing they said or did to each other meant anything.

'Because you gave him a second chance? Oh, he's grateful for that, but he can't help thinking I've sold myself to you for twenty-five thousand pounds,' she smiled bitterly. 'Quite a lot of money to pay for the body of one skinny teenager.'

Joel's jaw tightened and a pulse beat angrily in his throat. 'Your body is not for sale! And you are *not* skinny. Your body is beautiful—I should know.' His mouth had a bitter twist to it.

'How can you bring that up?' Farrah demanded tearfully.

'Why not?' he sat forward, his powerful shoulders blocking out the rest of the room, leaving his face the only thing in her vision. 'I can remember quite clearly what your body was like; smooth, and creamy, and infinitely kissable.'

Farrah shivered at the seduction in his voice. 'Stop it!' She shook her head. 'I don't want to listen to any more!'

'You may have to, Farrah. I wanted you. A fleeting emotion, but true nonetheless.'

Her eyes flew open to stare disbelievingly into the sleepy passion of Joel's narrowed eyes. 'You—you wanted me?' she repeated tremulously.

'Yes.' His hand covered the nervous movements of hers. 'Does that surprise you? It shouldn't,' he smiled mockingly. 'I don't usually make love to women I find unattractive.'

She gasped. 'You didn't make love to me!'

'No, but I could have. It was too soon, that's all. And it wasn't the right time for us.'

'It will never be the right time! Your mistress had just left the house after—well, after finding us together. And you were thinking of making love to me!'

'What else should I have been thinking of? All I could see or feel was you.'

'I hate you, Joel Falcone!' she told him in a furious whisper. 'You and your desire or indifference! I wish you felt indifference! I've told you before and I'll tell you again now, I will not be used! Now if you'll excuse me, I would like to leave.'

His hand tightened painfully on hers. 'I'm not ready to go yet.'

Her head flicked back angrily. 'I didn't ask you to. I'd rather go alone.'

'Oh no, you don't, Farrah,' he said tautly. 'You're not running out on me at the first obstacle.'

'You call wanting me an *obstacle*! I call it downright frightening.'

'This isn't the first time you've called me frightening. I don't understand the emotion.'

'You don't understand *any* emotion! That's the trouble.'

'I'm not the emotionless automaton you think I am. I thought I'd effectively proved that.' His words were self-derisory.

'All you proved was that you react normally to the female body. Congratulations!' she taunted, more hurt than she cared to admit. Joel had admitted finding her attractiveness enough to want her, but that wasn't what she wanted! She couldn't let him make love to her just through desire, it was against everything she held sacred.

'I didn't need you to prove that,' Joel said harshly.

'I know that. Look, Joel, we can't continue with this now, not now I know how you feel. I couldn't pretend —not knowing you, actually—I just can't do it any more!'

'Now that's a shame, because I think I'm going to find it easier.'

Farrah wrenched her hands out of his grasp, wishing he would move away from her and let her think straight. 'I can't do it, Joel!'

'No one's going to force you to do anything you don't want to,' he said calmly. 'You aren't indifferent to me, Farrah, you never have been.'

She stood up. 'I'm leaving. I won't stay here and listen to any more of this!'

He stood up too. 'And you aren't leaving without me either. We have a bargain, remember? And I aim to keep you to it.'

'Please, Joel, leave me alone.'

'That's the one thing I don't intend doing. Sit down, Farrah, and we'll talk.' He watched her through narrowed eyes as she slowly did as he asked, and then sat down himself. 'I had a telephone call from Laura today.'

Her eyes widened. 'You did?'

Joel lit up a cheroot before answering. 'Mmm. Very interesting it was too.'

'What—what did she say?' Farrah tried not to sound too interested. Joel was deliberately being evasive to make her curious. And the worst of it was, he was succeeding!

'Do you really want to know?'

'Of course I do. I'm involved in this too, remember?'

He gave a tight smile. 'I'm glad to hear it, for a while back there I thought you'd defected.'

'Joel! You're being infuriating!'

'Another of my faults. Laura wanted to know if you were still around. She even offered to stop interfering in my business life if I finished with you. She must think it's serious.'

'She—— She did that? What did you say to her?'

'What do you think I said? I only said *business* life, Farrah, her other plans still seem to be intact. And I'm not in love with her, I never have been. I should have realised this partnership was a mistake from the beginning, I just never expected her to take advantage of it. I don't like blackmail,' he said grimly.

Farrah gave an inward sigh of relief. She couldn't bear it if Joel went back to that she-cat. Laura Bennett was too much like Joel himself for them ever to be happy together; both were over-confident and arrogant, much too arrogant for their own good. But with the right person Joel could be different altogether, with someone he loved ...

'You haven't answered my question yet. Where were you last night?'

'Out,' she answered stubbornly. 'I don't question your whereabouts when you aren't with me.'

'I'd tell you if you bothered to ask me. I have nothing to hide. But *you* do. You were out with your boy-friend, weren't you, this Nigel you've been dating?'

She couldn't miss the dangerous glint in his steely blue eyes. 'And what if I were? It's nothing to do with you.'

'Nothing——! Good God, Farrah! I won't let you see him!' he declared haughtily.

'You can't stop me, Joel,' she told him defiantly. 'I—I—I love him!' The words were spoken before she could stop herself. She looked at him, stricken. How could she have said such a thing? It was an unforgivable lie.

His grasp on her wrist was so painful she almost cried out. 'I don't believe you, Farrah. Tell me it isn't tr——'

'Joel! I didn't realise you were here.' A hearty voice cut Joel off in mid-sentence, and they looked up to see the same man who had spoken to Joel the last time they were out for the evening. He came to stand next to their table, looking down at Farrah with frankly admiring eyes. 'And the beautiful Farrah,' he added deeply.

'Simon,' Joel returned tightly. He nodded to Simon's companion. 'Stella,' he added stiffly before looking back at Simon. 'I'm surprised you remember Farrah.'

Simon laughed softly. 'Couldn't forget her, much too charming to forget. I wish I knew where Joel's been hiding you,' he said to her alone.

Farrah blushed at his obvious interest in her. 'Why don't you ask him?' she suggested throatily, being deliberately provocative and watching Joel's face darken with anger at her action. If she didn't know better she would have said he was jealous. But that was a ridiculous idea, Joel didn't care enough about any woman to feel such a possessive emotion. 'Why don't you join us, Mr——?' she raised an eyebrow enquiringly.

'Just call me Simon,' he grinned at her, ignoring Joel's scowl. 'And we would love to join you, wouldn't we, Stella?'

The petite blonde had her china blue eyes fixed on Joel as he regarded her with mocking humour. 'Love to,' she replied huskily, seating herself in the vacant chair beside Joel as Simon sat next to Farrah. 'Order us all a drink, darling,' she told Simon.

'Sure. Joel?' Simon stopped a waiter and gave him their order before turning to Farrah, moving closer to her and resting his arm along the back of her chair. 'So where have you been all my life?' He smilingly held her gaze.

'Avoiding you, I should think,' drawled Joel.

'Joel darling,' Stella demanded his attention, 'you didn't come to my party on Saturday. It was quite flat without you.'

Farrah's mouth tightened as she saw the other girl's hand rest fleetingly on Joel's thigh. She had invited this couple to join them to make Joel angry, but it seemed to be having the opposite effect. He now seemed calm and mocking and *she* was the one getting angry, jealously so. Was this Stella another of Joel's women? Each one seemed to be more beautiful than the last, beautiful and sexy.

Stella was the sort of petite blonde Farrah had always wanted to be. The gown she wore was very thin and sheer, and Farrah felt sure the other girl wore little beneath it. Its blue colour perfectly matched her blue eyes, her matt complexion owing little to make-up and her lips were full and pouting.

Joel lit a cheroot, watching Stella through narrowed eyes. 'Don't tell me you actually noticed my absence,' he said lazily.

'But of course I did. Where were you?'

'I went to the country for the weekend.'

Simon attracted Farrah's attention by touching her hand. 'Do you live in London, Farrah?'

She wrenched her eyes away from the couple now huddled together, their conversation continuing in murmurs. 'Yes,' she answered him distractedly. 'I live with my father.'

'Do you work?'

She gave a light laugh. 'I'm not one of the idle rich. if that's what you mean.'

'So what do you do?' Simon seemed totally engrossed with her, and she had perforce to answer.

'I——' she glanced uncertainly at Joel, but he wasn't listening to them, a lazy smile on his face as he listened to the animated Stella. 'I work in an office. Nothing very exciting, I'm afraid.'

'You're exciting enough.'

She laughed at his effusive compliment. Simon was a sophisticated man in his own right, probably only two or three years Joel's junior, and yet he was the type of man Farrah could handle, with none of the dangerous charm Joel possessed. 'You're flattering me.'

'Not at all. You can always rely on Joel to come up with someone new and exciting.'

The smile faded from Farrah's lips. She didn't like being grouped with the many passing affairs Joel had participated in. 'I'm not new and exciting, I'm just an ordinary girl.'

Simon looked disbelieving. 'Not if Joel is interested in you.'

'And what makes you think he is?'

'This is the second time I've seen you with him, once

is enough to know if he likes you or not. Believe me, he likes you.'

'Believe *me*—he doesn't. Do you dance, Simon?'

He looked startled. 'I shuffle about a bit, which is all you can do on the floor space here. Are you asking me to dance, Farrah?'

'I—I suppose I must be.' Now what was she doing! Her tongue seemed to be running away from her this evening, and it was all to infuriate Joel. The couples dancing together here were as close as the other evening and she wondered what she had let herself in for, as Simon made no secret of his attraction to her.

'Do you realise, even though this is supposed to be the time of equality, that this is the first time a woman has asked me to dance?' He glanced at Joel. 'Is he going to mind?'

Nothing he said could have made her more determined. 'Why should he?' she asked carelessly. 'I'm capable of making my own decisions.'

'Okay then.' He stood up, holding out a hand to her to lead her on to the floor space, ignoring the sharp look directed at them from a stern-looking Joel. 'Excuse us,' he said swiftly.

He didn't hold her as close as Joel had, but it was close enough for her to feel uncomfortable in his arms. She pulled away slightly, and Simon looked down at her. 'Are you annoyed with Joel about something?' he asked curiously.

Farrah's eyes met his. 'What makes you think that?'

Simon laughed softly. 'I'm not stupid, Farrah. Your interest lies solely in Joel, and yet you asked me to dance. At a guess I would say you were having a slight argument when we arrived on the scene.'

She smiled unwillingly. 'Was it so obvious?'

'Only to me, I doubt Stella noticed anything. And if the looks Joel's sending in my direction are anything to go by I should say he's regretting it ever happened. He won't take kindly to my dancing with you.'

'I don't give a damn,' she said obstinately.

'Oh yes, you do. And I'm beginning to wish Rina would sing something with a bit more beat to it, at least if I danced away from you Joel might drop the scowl.'

'Rina?' Farrah queried.

'I realise Joel may be riveting company, but surely you've noticed there's a singer in here?' he teased.

'Oh—oh, yes,' she blushed. 'Don't worry about Joel, he doesn't care what I do.'

'Don't worry about Joel? You must be joking!' He looked down at the bracelet on her wrist as her hands rested on his shoulders. 'A present from Joel?'

Her lips tightened. 'Yes.'

'Very nice. It matches your eyes.'

'I know,' she said bitterly.

'Oh, I see. Joel already made that comment.'

Farrah hadn't been wearing the bracelet when she had met Joel this evening, but he had made her go back up to the flat to get it. She had mumbled something to her father about forgetting her purse before dashing out again. Her father knew nothing about the bracelet; as she intended returning it, one way or another, there seemed no point in telling him.

'Yes,' she told him stiffly.

'Oh dear, he is out of favour. Even more so in a moment, I should think, he and Stella are about to join us on the dance floor—and Stella makes no secret of her wish to share Joel's bed. She could just succeed with him in this mood.'

'Don't you mind—about Stella, I mean? After all, she is here with you.'

'Stella is my sister. We just called in here for an hour or so on our way to a party.' He looked over pointedly to where Stella was dancing as close to Joel as it was humanly possible to do without being obscene. 'But I somehow don't think she'll go now. Stella may not have realised you had an argument, but she certainly knows there's something wrong between the two of you, Joel's never taken this much interest in her before.'

'Stella is your *sister*?' she repeated hollowly.

'I'm afraid so. So don't count on me to divert her. I'm afraid you'll have to get his attention back by yourself. That shouldn't be too difficult.'

'What makes you think that?'

'The fact that he hasn't taken his eyes off you for the last quarter of an hour. I'm begining to feel uncomfortable.'

'Would you like to sit down?'

'Good idea.' He breathed a sigh of relief as they dropped into their seats. 'If I know Joel he'll be back at the table in a couple of minutes. You do realise you may have ruined an almost lifelong friendship?' he added ruefully.

Farrah looked guilty. 'I'm sorry. I didn't mean——'

'I'm only joking,' he grinned at her. 'He'll get over it—given time.'

She wasn't so sure. Joel would be livid with her over this evening, and while she might have seen him annoyed in the past she had never yet seen him furiously angry. The evening had started off wrongly, with Joel ordering her to wear the bracelet, and it had gone from bad to worse.

'Hey, don't worry.' Simon took her hand. 'Joel can't eat you. He must realise you're only flirting with me out of pique.'

Not when she had just told him she was in love with Nigel! If only he hadn't forbidden her to see Nigel she would never have told him that lie, she would have told him that she and Nigel had parted company. But she would not be ordered about by Joel; he had things enough his own way without that. But there was no doubt in her mind that she would pay for her treatment of him this evening, and she had probably ruined any of their efforts to give the impression they were in love with each other—something else he wouldn't thank her for.

'They're coming back to the table now, Farrah,' Simon told her softly. He let go of her hand at the dark brooding look in his friend's eyes. 'Are you ready to leave now, Stella?' he asked his sister loudly.

Stella looked at him coldly. 'Don't be silly, Simon, I'm having much too—interesting a time here.'

Simon stood up determinedly. 'I think we should go, Stella. We've broken up Farrah and Joel's evening enough as it is. And Maggie's expecting us.'

His sister's face dropped with disappointment. 'I suppose so.' Her eyes brightened. 'I don't suppose the two of you would like to come too?' Her question was directed at Joel, and Farrah knew that as far as the other girl was concerned she might as well not be here.

This time Joel didn't consult her. 'I don't think so, Stella. It's already ten-thirty, by the time we reach Maggie's it'll be nearly eleven.'

'But that's early! Don't be such a grouch, Joel.'

He smiled at her, and Farrah held her breath as she waited for his answer. 'Some of us have to be at work at nine o'clock in the morning. We can't all spend the morning in bed.'

Stella put her hand on his arm encouragingly. 'Just come along for an hour or so. To make up for Saturday,' she added silkily.

Joel laughed at her pouting expression. 'You must have been a very spoilt little girl!'

Her eyes brightened. 'You mean you'll come? Oh, that's lovely!'

'Only for an hour or so. Farrah has a job of work to do tomorrow, and as her boss I demand she be in on time.'

Farrah stiffened at his last taunting words. 'I'm never late,' she told him angrily, her eyes flashing as he looked at her mockingly. Oh, how he was enjoying this revenge on her! They said revenge was sweet, and Joel certainly looked pleased about something.

Simon raised surprised eyebrows. 'Then you work for Joel?'

She smiled at him, ignoring the fact that Joel and Stella were now waiting for her to leave with them. 'Does that surprise you?'

'Nothing about Joel surprises me. Come to the party, Farrah. I'd like you to.'

She jumped as she felt Joel's hand slide slowly down her arm and his fingers entwine intimately with hers. She could feel the warmth of his body close beside her and anything she might have been going to say in answer to Simon flew completely out of her mind. She could think of nothing but Joel, and the way his thumb was caressing the back of her hand. 'I—I——' she licked her lips nervously.

'Sure she'll come,' Joel answered for her smoothly. 'But because *I* want her to.'

She looked at him wordlessly, but his eyes were still shuttered from her and she knew he was still angry with her. And probably with good cause. She had behaved childishly, and dared she say it—jealously. She only hoped Joel didn't realise this was the emotion that had prompted her behaviour, what had made her falsely declare her love for Nigel, and flirt openly with Simon. She was jealous even of a telephone conversation with Laura, and she knew she had fallen irrevocably in love with him.

He was the opposite of everything she had ever desired in a man, arrogant, experienced, and most of all, cynical. And yet it had happened! And it was becoming more and more true every time she saw him. She was learning that love couldn't be denied merely at will, it flourished even when vehemently pushed aside.

'Honey?' Joel was looking at her strangely, and Stella didn't look too happy about Farrah regaining his attention. 'We're ready to leave.'

She snapped herself out of her thoughts, conscious that Joel still held her hand firmly enmeshed with his own. 'Yes,' she said dazedly.

Stella, not to be outdone, threaded her hand through Joel's other arm, her scarlet-painted fingernails holding on to his blue velvet dinner jacket. 'Can I drive there with you, darling?'

He shook his head. 'We'll meet you there.'

'Oh, but——'

Simon pulled her firmly away, glaring down angrily at his very determined sister. 'We'll meet them there, Stella,' he told her firmly. 'Do you usually desert your partner this early in the evening? I wouldn't have brought you if I'd known.'

'And I wouldn't have come with you at all if my car weren't out of action.'

He grinned. 'Ungrateful brat!'

The two couples parted in the car park and Farrah waited expectantly for Joel's criticism of her. Amazingly he said very little, keeping his conversation to general subjects until Farrah thought she could stand no more. Now she knew how Nigel had felt the evening before when waiting for her to tell him about her friendship with Joel. And it wasn't a pleasant feeling, in fact she felt as if she would scream any moment now.

'Joel——' her voice came out shakily and she cursed herself for being a coward. It wouldn't do for her to become too pliable in his hands, not now, when she

knew how easily he could make her a willing recipient
to his caressing hands. 'Joel,' she said more firmly.

'Yes?' His eyes remained narrowed on the road.

'Joel, we can't go on like this. No one is going to believe we love each other if we treat each other with dislike.'

'Do you care?' he asked harshly.

Did she care! She *loved* him. 'Not for myself,' she
lied. 'But I thought you were set on everyone believing
it.'

'And you seem to be equally determined that *no one*
believes it. Your behaviour tonight has been nothing
less than disgraceful.'

'*My* behaviour!' Farrah interrupted him. 'You were
allowing Stella liberties on the dance floor that should
be confined to a bedroom,' she said in disgust.

'I'm sure Stella would have preferred we use a bedroom too,' he acknowledged mockingly.

'You're disgusting!'

'And you're a flirt!' His eyes flickered over her scathingly. 'Only seconds after telling me you love someone
called Nigel you begin to encourage Simon in a way
that can only be construed as an invitation. I'm surprised he didn't make more of it. Or have you arranged
to meet him some other time?'

'And you said I have a low opinion of you!' she derided.

'Well, have you?' he persisted in his question.

'Don't be silly. Simon was kind to me, that's all.'

'Everyone seems to like being kind to you, first
George and now Simon. And what were you talking to
Simon about?'

'You,' she answered truthfully.

'Me? I see. And what did you decide between the
two of you? That I'm a cold unfeeling swine who
doesn't deserve you?' he laughed throatily. 'But then

I don't *have* you, do I? Do you think Simon realised that? I'm sure he noticed your eyes.'

'These damned unawakened eyes! No, he didn't realise that you hadn't made love to me. Why should he? The prowess of Joel Falcone can never be doubted, can it? You told me at the beginning that no woman was considered safe with you. Why should Simon think I would be any different, that you would expect less from me than from any other woman?' The words were meant to hurt and she knew they had angered him as he veered off into a side road and brought the car to a halt before turning to her.

'And if I did expect that of you? What would you do? Give in like you have over every other demand I've made of you?' His eyes gleamed challengingly in the darkness. 'Would you even sacrifice that for your father?'

'Stop it, Joel! Please, stop it. You've been so cruel to me this evening. I hate it. I hate it, I tell you!' Tears gathered in her eyes and for the first time since this dreadful business began she felt as if she were going to cry, deep racking sobs that would erase all the bitterness and replace it with love. But that was impossible, Joel would never love her!

For answer he pulled her into his arms, cradling her head gently against his shoulder. 'I forget what a sensitive little thing you are, Farrah,' he said huskily, his warm breath fanning the soft tendrils of hair on her forehead. 'Just when I think you're about to tell me exactly what you think of me, you act hurt and I feel like a heel.'

Farrah sniffed tearfully. 'I'm not acting, Joel. You seem to think that every thing I do has a double meaning.'

'Experience,' he murmured close to her ear. 'You have a fragrance all your own,' he told her, bending his head to bury his face in her slender throat. 'I never believed I would fall for the innocence and sweetness routine,' he continued musingly. 'But you have it off to a fine art. You're getting under my skin, Farrah, and I'm afraid that pretty soon I'm going to have to do something about it.'

'What—what do you mean?' Her startled gaze rested on his bent head.

'I mean that I'm going to have to make love to you.' He pulled away from her to look into her face, his mouth only inches away from her own. 'Does that frighten you, honey?'

'Don't keep calling me that!' she snapped, trying to bring a little sanity into the conversation. 'We don't have any witnesses now.'

His thumb caressed her lips apart and he played with the soft sweetness of her mouth. 'I'm beginning to think I don't need an audience when you're about, in fact, I would welcome a little privacy. I think we'll give the party a miss and go to my apartment instead.'

'No!' she said sharply. 'I want to go home. It's late, and I don't like being mocked. I think this whole thing has gone far enough! You said at the start that you weren't personally interested in me, but now you've decided I might prove an interesting diversion. I'm conveniently here, you have a hold over me, so why not take advantage of the situation! That's the way you're thinking, isn't it, Joel?' She pushed his caressing hands away. 'Well, I've had enough! You can find someone else to taunt. I don't care what you do any more, but I will not be a party to this charade any longer.'

Joel sat back, completely unmoved by her outburst. 'You're intriguing, Farrah,' he drawled, playing with a soft shiny wave at her nape. 'But I'm afraid it's too late to back out now, much too late. I no longer have a hold over you, your father's—error has been cleared and the books now stand correct. But tonight you've made this *charade*, as you call it, irreversible.'

'*I* have? What did I do?'

He smiled at her puzzled frown, that cynical smile that Farrah hated—and yet loved. 'Simon may be a friend of mine, but he is also the owner of *Success* magazine, and has connections with all the big newspapers, hence our friendship. Thanks to your talking and acting as you did with him I would say it's a certainty that an article about the two of us will appear in a lot of the evening papers tomorrow, and in the dailies the day after.'

CHAPTER EIGHT

'Oh, no!' Her face was stricken.

Joel chuckled. 'Oh, yes.'

'But why didn't you stop me?' she flared at him accusingly. 'I didn't realise Simon's connections, but *you* did. You could have warned me.'

He restarted the car, moving it out into the traffic before answering her. 'Why should I? I knew that sooner or later you would rebel, and now you've irrevocably linked your name with mine you're going to find it harder than ever to back out.'

'You knew this would happen. You *knew!*' she said fiercely.

'Guilty,' he admitted. 'I conveniently mentioned your name to Simon the other evening in the hope that he would remember you. It was unfortunate that he came across us tonight as we were arguing—at least, I *thought* it was. It actually seemed to convince him more. A lovers' tiff,' he mocked.

'This is terrible,' she shook her head. 'I never imagined anything like this happening. Can't you stop him?'

'Maybe, but I'm not going to try,' he declared adamantly.

'I see.'

He glanced at her fleetingly, chuckling lightly. 'Don't look so tight-mouthed, Farrah. This is exactly what we wanted, a definite show of our relationship.'

'What *you* wanted, you mean. Why can't you just go about things normally like anyone else? Why do you have to go to all this trouble? I'm sure that if you both sat down and discussed this reasonably, you could come to some kind of agreement.'

'You think so? Why don't we just try asking her, she should be at this party.'

'Oh no, now that's asking too much! I don't have to be humiliated in front of Miss Bennett a second time. I would prefer to go home.'

'Mine?'

'No, not yours! Don't you ever give up?'

'No,' he laughed.

Farrah loved to see him laugh, it was something that didn't happen too often, and she watched him with pleasure, finally smiling with him. 'I really would prefer to go home.'

'Right.'

Strangely Farrah felt disappointed. Joel had agreed too readily. 'Will you—will you still go to the party?'

'I guess so.'

'Oh,' she said dully. There was no doubt that Joel would spend the rest of the evening with Stella. She found herself heartily disliking the other girl. The thought of Joel making love to another woman made her feel ill, and the thought of him even *talking* to Stella made her feel angry.

Joel glanced at her. 'What do you mean, eh? That prudish little mind of yours is working overtime,' he sneered. 'Whose bed do you think I'll be sharing tonight? Stella's or Laura's? God, what a mind you have! You're beginning to sound like my wife!'

'Spare me that!' she retorted, stung by the scorn in his voice. 'If any woman ever makes the mistake of becoming your wife then I'll pity her.' Why did she say these things? Why did she hurt herself, because it was a sure fact Joel was unmoved by any of her verbal outbursts? She was only punishing herself, and it was a pain she found unbearable. If only she didn't love him so much!

His eyes taunted her. 'She'll probably need it. You're the faithful type, aren't you?'

'Yes. Boring, isn't it?' She too could be mocking.

'Unusual, rather than boring.'

'You're so cynical, Joel. A lot of people are faithful to each other all their lives. Have you never loved anyone, not anyone at all?'

'Only my family.'

'Your family?' Somehow she had never fitted him into a family unit, which was rather ridiculous of her; he must have had a family at some time, even if he seemed a solitary figure now.

'I guess to you I must seem as if I came straight from the devil,' he said dryly. 'But my mother wouldn't be very pleased to hear it. She's the only woman I know that loves me for myself and not for what I can give her.'

'Your mother is still alive?' She couldn't help her surprise.

'Mmm, she still lives in the area we lived in when I was a kid. I have a kid brother too. He's in advertising.' This was the first time he had talked about his family, and Farrah had the feeling he had not intended to do so now. He gave a harsh laugh. 'I guess you wouldn't think Richie such a kid, he's twenty-five. I'll introduce you to him some time. On second thoughts, I take back that remark, I never share what I covet.'

'Does he live in London?' Her cheeks were flushed from his renewed mention of his desire for her.

'Sometimes. He commutes between the States and here. He'll probably be back here next week. Have you heard enough about my family now? Or would you like to go to my apartment and see some family photographs?'

'Oh no,' she laughed. 'I may be innocent, but I'm not that naïve. Family photographs are a replacement for etchings, I gather?'

'You gather correct. It's eleven-thirty, you'd better go in now. I'll call you. All right?'

'All right,' she answered huskily.

Joel moved slowly, his lips parting her mouth with a kiss that caressed rather than took, asking for a response but not demanding one. She moved into his arms, loving the possessive feel of his hands on her body, arching her neck as he probed the sensitive area of her throat with his tongue.

'God, Farrah, I could kiss you all night!' he murmured into the softness of her hair. 'But that isn't possible, is it?'

Wordlessly she shook her head, her parted lips all the invitation Joel needed to continue his exploration of her mouth. She became lost in time, conscious only of a need for Joel to continue these long drugging kisses and for his hands to know her body intimately. Her own hands were below his velvet jacket, touching his muscled back and feeling the heat of his body through the silk shirt.

She could hear the ragged breathing in his throat—or was it her own?—she didn't know any more. She smoothed back the dark hair from his forehead, revelling in her power to arouse him. This was where she belonged, where she longed to be whenever she was with him.

Joel's eyes were half-closed with passion as he leant back against the car door. 'We don't seem to be able to strike a happy medium, Farrah. Last time it was the right place but the wrong time, this time it's the wrong place at the right time. You won't change your mind and come back with me?'

She shook her head, her emotions still too high for her to answer sensibly. The trouble was she didn't want to be sensible, she wanted to throw herself into Joel's arms and go home with him, even though she knew the inevitable outcome. Joel might not be able to love her as she wanted him to, but there could be no doubt in her mind, or body, that he would not be a selfish lover. The weekend spent at his home had more than proved that. He had been intent only on arousing her, his own desire held firmly in check until her own needs equalled his. And if he hadn't spoken she would probably not have come to her senses until it was too late.

But she had been sensible! And she had to be the same now. She couldn't weaken, even though Joel's eyes beckoned her to follow her senses, and not her mind. 'It's late,' came her quiet reply. 'You said you would call me?'

'Mm. Goodnight, honey, and don't think I've given up. I think the only way to get you out of my mind is to take you to my bed. I've never known any woman live up to my first expectations of her, and consequently I've learnt to expect little, that way I'm not disappointed. And, Farrah ...'

She looked at him anxiously. 'Yes?'

'I'm not going to the party.' Again his thumb moved compulsively to part her lips. 'Stella's cloying beauty after you could prove a letdown I don't need.' He straightened in his seat. 'Now off you go to your virtuous bed.'

'Don't mock, Joel. Not now.'

'Okay, baby. But go now—or I could just change my mind and simply take you with me. It would be so easy, Farrah,' he warned.

'I'm going, I'm going!'

'I thought you might,' he said dryly.

Farrah scrambled out of the car, and with one last wave of her hand she slowly entered the flat. Her father was still up when she got in, and after making them both a quick coffee she went straight to her bedroom. But not to sleep. Her mind and body were still so full of Joel that she couldn't relax. His desire for her was no longer a guessed-at thing, but a stated fact. Her body tingled with the knowledge of it.

But she was rather distressed about Simon. Would he really give the story of their romance to the newspapers? Joel said yes, and she had perforce to believe him, after all he knew Simon better than she did. It was rather a frightening thought, to have her name linked with Joel's in the public press, to be read about by thousands of people who had never heard of Farrah Halliday, but must surely be familiar with the name of Joel Falcone.

Farrah's face was fiery red and her eyes downcast. Angie had warned her that things could become difficult for her in the office, and today was the worst. And who could blame them! She had been more than shocked herself this morning when she had seen the newspaper her father subscribed to, and her father had been horrified. Emblazoned across the front of the daily newspaper was a photograph of herself and Joel as they had left the Falcone building for lunch the day before. As promised, Joel had telephoned her and they had met at twelve-thirty yesterday. But neither of them could have guessed that a photographer was waiting patiently outside for just such an occurrence. Unfortunately for Farrah, and fortunately for the photographer, he had caught them just as Joel was opening the car door for her and she was laughing up happily into his face.

To anyone reading the newspaper, she and Joel looked exactly what they were described as, 'very good friends'. Her father had almost choked over his morning cup of tea when he saw the article, and although he didn't say a great deal she knew he expected less notorious behaviour from her. Her parents had always tried never to interfere in decisions concerning her private life although they had insisted that she obtain a good education. But in the case of Joel Falcone, Farrah knew her father ached to put a stop to her seeing him, and she also knew he would never attempt to do so.

Even if Farrah were free to tell her father of the reasons behind her seeing Joel she knew it would no longer be true. It no longer applied. She wasn't seeing Joel because she had to, but because she *wanted* to. And she knew the situation had changed for Joel too. No longer did he treat her with mocking condescension, but more with the patient indulgence of a man who is sure he will get what he wants in the end. And he wanted her. There could be no doubt about it, it was there in every touch, and the warmth of his eyes spoke of a slumbering passion that only needed one word from her to make it spark into an engulfing ecstasy. And that one word was, yes.

The reaction of the girls in the department to the newspaper report was obvious as soon as she walked into the office. The buzz of conversation stopped instantly, and she had to walk to her desk under the close scrutiny of nine pairs of eyes. And it had continued like this for the past couple of hours, the only one seeming to be her usual friendly self being Fiona.

She joined Farrah as usual for their coffee-break, observing Farrah's pale tense face with sympathy. 'You've done it now, love,' she said teasingly. 'Your friendship with Mr Falcone is no longer a company secret.'

Farrah grimaced, aware that they were being closely observed by the other girls, discreetly, but nevertheless observed. 'It was never intended to be. Joel couldn't give a damn about other people's opinion of him, or anything he does.'

'But you could. It's all right for Mr Falcone, he's sitting in his office on the fifteenth floor with not a care in the world, but you—you have to sit down here and take the barbed criticism of a lot of cats, hypocritical cats at that. None of them would have acted any differently in the same circumstances. I know I wouldn't. Your Mr Falcone is one hell of a man. And the sexy way he calls you honey! It sent shivers down my spine!'

Farrah laughed for the first time that day. 'He isn't *my* Mr Falcone, he isn't *anyone's* Mr Falcone, he never will be.'

'I suppose not, but he——'

Fiona was cut off in mid-sentence as the telephone on Farrah's desk began to ring persistently. With a grimace in Fiona's direction, and a regretful look at her half-drunk coffee that was sure to be cold by the time the telephone conversation was over, she picked up the receiver, reciting her extension number habitually.

'Honey?'

Fiona was right, the way Joel said that was definitely sexy, and it sent shivers down *her* spine too. 'Yes,' she replied huskily, conscious of Fiona sitting only a few feet away.

'Can you talk?'

'No.'

'Well, can you come up here?'

'No, I can't do that either,' she said firmly. There was enough gossip being spread about them today without adding to it.

'You sound upset,' Joel guessed perceptively. 'Is anything wrong?'

Was anything wrong! *Everything* was wrong, from her first meeting with him to this newspaper article. 'Why should there be?' she asked casually.

'Because there is. I can tell when you're upset. I have to talk to you about something important, so you either come up here or I come down to you. It's urgent that I see you now. So, which is it to be?'

'Neither. I'm working right now. Perhaps we can talk later.' She was trying so hard to make this conversation seem like a normal telephone call, but everything she did at the moment seemed suspect to the girls in the office with her, and she knew they probably guessed it was Joel she was talking to. 'I really do have a lot to do.'

She saw Fiona glance sceptically at the small pile of letters on her desk which had to be answered, and blushed guiltily. 'Would you like me to leave?' mouthed Fiona, and Farrah furiously shook her head.

'I mean it, Farrah,' Joel's voice came sure and firm to her through the receiver. 'I'll be down there in five minutes.'

'No!' she said sharply. 'I—— It's all right, I can be there myself in the same time.'

'Make sure you are,' he warned, before she heard the firm click of the receiver.

'The man himself?' enquired Fiona lightly, standing to smooth her skirt.

Farrah blushed. Joel was making things more difficult for her than she had ever imagined. She had realised that many people would know about them, but she hadn't quite realised what effect this was going to have on her career. Already she had lost the chance of being transferred to one of the reporting sections, something she had always wanted, and she wondered what other far-reaching effects it was going to have on her life.

Consequently, she was not in the best of humour by the time she entered Joel's secretary's office, Cathy's smile of greeting disappearing as she saw the scowl on her face. 'Mr Falcone is expecting you,' she said smoothly.

'I know,' mumbled Farrah.

'Oh dear,' laughed Cathy.

Farrah smiled reluctantly. 'Sorry. I'm feeling a bit touchy today.'

'I know the feeling. I should go straight in, he isn't with anyone at the moment.'

'Thanks.' Farrah didn't bother to knock on the door, but walked straight in. Joel was studying some papers on his desk, but at her entrance he placed them away in a folder to sit back and watch her through narrowed eyes. She remained unmoved by his look, walking purposefully across the room to stand in front of him. 'You sent for me—sir.' There was no mistaking the defiance in her voice and she saw his eyes narrow even more.

'The first time I asked,' he pointed out reasonably. 'The second time I ordered.'

'Well, I'm here, aren't I?'

He stood up to move around his desk, dressed formally in a grey pin-striped suit and snowy white shirt that emphasised the darkness of his skin colouring. 'So, what's happened to put you in this foul mood?'

'What's happened! The newspapers are what's happened! Our picture smeared all over the front page of most of the daily newspapers. As if there aren't enough catastrophes in the world for them to write about, without resorting to such trivialities as news!'

'Scandal *is* news,' Joel said dryly, his arms folded across his chest as he leant back against his desk. 'Or didn't you know?'

'But not front page news!'

'To my competitors it is.' His mouth curved into a mocking smile. 'They think it will damage my business reputation to be seen apparently besotted with a teenager.'

Farrah's eyes widened. 'And will it?'

'I doubt it. I'm not exactly the type of man to go soft over a woman, and most people know that. And why are you so annoyed about the picture? I did warn you what would happen a couple of days ago.'

'I know that.' She turned away from the attractive picture he made to stare out of the window. He disturbed her too much this close. 'But all the girls in my office saw the newspapers, and I'm being treated like something rather nasty at the moment.'

'They'll get over it. Our "romance",' his mouth twisted mockingly, 'our romance will be a nine-day wonder. Everyone will soo forget about it, and life will go on as normal.'

'You think so?' Her green eyes sparkled angrily. 'For you maybe, but not for me. Already it's upset my father, all the people who work here treat me like a stranger, and the worst of it is, it's ruined any immediate plans for my career, whether that will be permanently I'm not sure.'

His mouth tightened. 'How has it done that?'

'Angie was going to have me transferred. I was actually going to get the chance to be a reporter.'

'So how did I ruin that for you?'

'Surely it's obvious, Joel. Angie can't move me now, it would look like favouritism. Surely you can see that?'

'Not really. Angie is a completely fair person, if she thinks you have something then you have something. She wouldn't allow something like this to influence her either way.'

'You know that, and I know that, but unfortunately not everyone else does. So it's all been cancelled.'

'I see. Would you like me to make a few telephone calls and get it all moving again?'

Farrah turned on him angrily. 'No, I wouldn't! I'll probably have to leave Falcone's in the end anyway. Once we stop seeing each other I should think I'll have everyone gloating over my loss of favour.'

Joel moved to turn and look out over the rooftops of London. 'And what happens if you don't?' he asked almost inaudibly.

'Don't what?' She looked at his broad back, her face puzzled.

'Stop seeing me,' he supplied impatiently.

'But—well, I—— But I will! As soon as this is over

it will be as if we've never met. We're unlikely to meet by accident socially, and I'll no longer be working for you. So the likelihood of our meeting is more or less nil.'

He turned to face her and she watched the play of muscles across his face. 'Not if we've arranged to meet,' he said stiffly.

'Now that isn't likely, is it——' she was stopped by the look on his face, his head thrown back almost challengingly. 'Is it?' she asked huskily, almost hesitantly.

'Why not?' Joel shrugged. 'I always like to get what I want.'

'I see.'

'Do you? I doubt it, I'm not sure that I exactly "see" myself. Will you go out with me if I ask you?'

Farrah couldn't help but smile, although the situation didn't really call for amusement. 'That would certainly be a novelty, up until now I haven't been given any choice in the matter.'

'True. We'll leave that for now, it won't happen for a couple of weeks anyway. For now I want to talk to you about my imminent trip to the States.'

'Oh no!' Her exclamation was an involuntary reflex, and she saw his start of surprise.

'What do you mean, oh no?'

'Well, I—— It—— It—— Well, it isn't convenient.'

'I'm so sorry,' he said sarcastically. 'What other plans did you have in mind for me?'

'Don't be mean, Joel. If you leave me now I'll have to face all those curious looks on my own.' She looked at him anxiously. 'I can't do it, Joel.'

'Why not?'

She looked at his cold impersonal face and gritted her teeth to hold back her angry retort. 'Because it isn't fair of you to leave me here with all these rumours circulating about us.'

'Then come with me.'

'Come with you?' she squeaked. 'But you—you can't mean it!'

'Damn it, of course I mean it! Do you think I want to leave you here? Don't be so damned silly.' His face had darkened angrily. 'So why not come with me? I have to be there for about a week, but I won't be working all the time. We could spend the evenings together. And the nights.'

'But I—— We couldn't do that!' Her thoughts were all confused, with a longing to go with him and the knowledge that she couldn't. What would everyone think if she up and left for the States with Joel? What would her father think? 'Is this just another ploy to get your freedom?'

'If you like to think so,' Joel said tightly. 'Well, are you coming or aren't you?'

'What a gracious invitation! And no, I'm not! I'm staying right here in England. I will not be seen to run away from anything.'

He moved forward to grasp her arms painfully. 'Is that what you think I'm doing? Running away?'

Of course she didn't think any such thing, but she preferred him to be this cold arrogant stranger rather than put up with the almost loverlike manner he had adopted with her of late. It would be all too easy to fall for his blatant masculinity and sensuous charm when he was in that type of mood, and she had no intention of making their supposed relationship a reality. No matter how much she longed to do just that.

She shook her head. 'No, I don't believe that.' But the words didn't sound very convincing, and this was intentionally so.

Joel shook her hard. 'I am not running away! I thought you knew me better than that. There's been some trouble in the American division. Believe me, I don't want to go—I would much rather stay here with you. While I'm away you'll have time to build up your defences again.'

Farrah pushed his arms away. 'I wasn't aware that I had any defences to lower. And if you must go to America, don't let me try and stop you.'

'It's started already, I see,' he taunted.

'Nothing has started! I've always disliked you, and you know it.'

To her surprise she heard him laugh, a deep mocking laugh that took him away from her across the room. 'If you choose to believe that then for the moment I'll let you. I don't have the time to prove otherwise. I have a lot to do before I leave, a lot of people to see.'

'Then I must be grateful for the fact that you had time to see me at all!'

Joel swung her round, his eyes steely. 'I would hardly leave *without* seeing you. Especially after this morning's newspapers. Laura is ever so slightly annoyed about it.'

Farrah's eyes widened. 'You've seen her?'

'She telephoned. About an hour ago, she must have thought it important to have got out of bed this time of morning. And the names she called you weren't polite,' he added with some amusement.

'She called *me*?' Farrah was astounded. 'What have *I* done?'

He touched her flushed cheeks, cradling each side of her face as he looked down at her. 'Stolen me from her,' he said softly.

'I haven't! I——'

'Quiet, child!' His dark head bent and he took possession of her lips. All Farrah's senses told her to resist, but her traitorous body betrayed her yet again. He pulled her against the hard length of his body, moulding her soft curves against his full arousal, only lifting his head to trail his lips across her shoulder and down to the dark shadow of her breasts. Against her will her breasts bloomed under his caress and she gasped her pleasure, her head thrown back, her eyes closed.

'Now tell me you haven't stolen me,' Joel groaned. 'And if you say it you'll be lying.'

He pulled her down into one of the leather armchairs intent only on kissing her until she forgot all else, drugging her senses as he had on Saturday night, and setting her body afire with wanting—wanting him in the truest sense between a man and woman.

'Oh God, Farrah!' He quivered against her with the effort it cost him not to take her here and now. 'You're a witch, you have to be.'

Farrah nibbled his ear lobe, uncaring for the moment what construction he would put on her actions. All she knew was that she wouldn't be seeing him for a week, maybe more, and she *needed* this—this being in his arms and feeling wanted as only Joel could make her feel.

He claimed her lips again, her vest top no barrier against his questing hands, and her moans of pleasure only inciting him more. The rosy tips of her breasts were like twin jewels and they attracted Joel like a magnet, his lips caressing and gentle.

Finally it was the buzzing of the intercom that broke them apart, Farrah moving almost guiltily, only to be stopped by Joel's hold on her. 'Don't leave me again, Farrah, not after this.'

'Leave you?' she repeated shakily. 'But of course I have to leave you.'

'Maybe bodily—for a while,' he murmured huskily. 'But don't shut me out again. I want to say more,' he looked up irritatedly as the intercom buzzed again, 'but I don't have the time. We'll leave it until I get back. Have you seen this boy Nigel again?' he asked sternly.

'N-Nigel?' Farrah was still dazed and shaken from their lovemaking. She had allowed Joel to touch her as no one else had ever done, and yet it had felt right, oh, so deliciously right.

'In that case, you haven't. Don't, Farrah. I'll rip him apart if he dares to come near you. I mean it, Farrah.'

And miraculously she knew he did. And this was the man who had professed never to feel possessive about any woman. Her smile was uncertain, a new hopeful feeling invaded her every thought. 'You don't need to worry in that direction,' she told him. 'Nigel bowed out of my life in a most gentlemanly fashion. He considered the competition too strong, namely you.'

'Good,' he said with a certain amount of satisfaction. 'Let's keep it that way.' He stood up, watching her with passionately sleepy eyes as she straightened her clothing, before walking over to the intercom. 'Yes?' he said tersely, his eyes still on Farrah.

'I have Miss Bennett on the line, Mr Falcone,' Cathy said breathlessly. 'I wouldn't have—er—interrupted, but Miss Bennett seemed very insistent. She said the matter was urgent.'

Joel's mouth twisted with mocking humour. 'Everything seems urgent to Laura, Cathy, you should know that. Put her through in exactly one minute.'

'Yes, sir.'

He turned to Farrah, his smile for her alone, the look in his eyes enough to turn her legs to jelly. 'I wonder if Laura realised just what she interrupted,' he teased. 'You're adorable, do you know that? And we'll have to continue this—conversation, when I return. Don't forget where it was interrupted.'

CHAPTER NINE

'So lover-boy has gone back to America,' commented her father.

They had just eaten their dinner the day after she and Joel had parted, and Farrah had eaten sparingly, her thoughts all of Joel and his return.

'Yes,' she said miserably, wishing with all her heart that it wasn't true.

'Did you see him for lunch before he left?' her father continued.

'For lunch?' she asked vaguely.

'Mmm, I thought that as you didn't see him last night perhaps you met him for lunch today as you sometimes do. Or is this friendship coming to an end?' His eyes lit up hopefully.

'No—no!' she said jerkily. 'What makes you think Joel left this afternoon?'

'The airline ticket requested dated for today. You can't keep much a secret in a big place like Falcone's. He left on the three o'clock flight.'

Joel had left *today*! So why had he said goodbye to her *yesterday*? More to the point, who had he been with last night? 'He—I—— We said goodbye in the morning.' And it wasn't a lie, except that it had been yesterday morning!

'I see. I had hoped that perhaps this separation would be a permanent thing.'

'It could be, Daddy.' She stood up with jerky movements, intent only on making her escape to the privacy of her bedroom. 'This separation will show if our feelings are of the lasting kind, won't it? I—er—I think I'll go to my room and read for a while.'

'All right, love. But you're not to mope about your room while Falcone's out of the country,' he warned. 'How can you give yourself a fair chance of forgetting about him if you stay in your room thinking about him all the time?'

'I didn't say I intended intentionally forgetting him, Daddy.' Forget Joel? Impossible! 'This is just a test.'

'Hmph,' mumbled her father. 'Fellow's not good enough for you. Dragging your name through the papers. Selfish, that's what he is, thinking only of himself and——' he looked at her sharply. 'Farrah, you haven't—the two of you haven't——'

'No, we haven't,' she said firmly, thanking God it was true, it could so easily have been otherwise. 'I can look after myself, Daddy.'

'Not with his sort you can't, you just aren't in his league when it comes to things like that. I should think he's lost count of the women who have shared his bed.'

'Well, I'm not one of them!' Farrah snapped, and then looked instantly contrite as she saw her father's hurt look. 'I'm sorry, Daddy. It's just that——'

He put a hand over hers understandingly. 'It's all right, love, no need to apologise. I shouldn't be interfering.'

'You're not interfering, you're just concerned, I know that. But I—I'm not sure how this relationship with Joel is going to end, or when. I'm all confused at the moment.'

'I realise that, love, and my going on at you isn't going to help. Off you go to your room, I won't mention him again until you feel like talking about him.'

'Okay, Daddy.'

The telephone rang in the hallway as she walked past and she picked it up, reciting their number. 'Farrah Halliday speaking,' she added.

'It's Nigel, Farrah. I wondered if you felt like coming out for a drink tonight?'

'Tonight? But I——'

'You aren't going out somewhere else, are you? Mr Falcone's away, isn't he?'

'Yes, he is, but what difference does that make?'

'Well, I thought that as he's away——'

'Yes? Just what did you think? That while the cat's away the little mouse will play?' she bit out at him angrily.

'Don't be silly, Farrah. As a *friend*, I thought you might be lonely. Forgive me if I presumed too much,' he added sarcastically, his voice chilling into anger, and Farrah knew she had hurt him deeply. He had only been trying to be nice, and anger was how she repaid him.

'I'm sorry, Nigel,' she gave a choked laugh. 'It seems to be my evening for snapping at people. I've just bitten poor Daddy's head off. Now what did you say about a drink?'

Half an hour later she and Nigel were firmly ensconced in a secluded corner of a little tavern they had often frequented during their three-month friendship. Farrah felt more relaxed with him than she ever did with Joel, and yet there was none of that tense excitement she always felt in Joel's company. Nigel was nice, and lots of fun, but she knew now that wasn't enough to evoke love. No, love came unbidden, and unwanted, and in completely the wrong direction, like her love for Joel.

'How's your father now?' Nigel took a huge gulp of his beer. 'Is he back at work?'

'Hmm, and loving it.'

'Has he got over the worry he had?' Nigel watched closely for her reaction.

Farrah evaded his eyes, her expression remaining calm with effort. She hadn't mentioned anything to him about the trouble they were having! 'Daddy's fine,' she answered tremulously. 'He was just ill after Mummy's death, we were both depressed, that's only natural. They were very much in love.'

'I know, Farrah. But your dad told me he had something else on his mind, some worry at work. Is that all sorted out now?'

'Yes, I guess so. I—he hasn't said anything, so I suppose it must be.'

'You're keeping something back, Farrah. Your father had something really big on his mind, something to do with Falcone's. Now I've been putting two and two together, and I——'

'You've made five,' she derided. 'People usually do when they let their imagination run riot. Whatever it was that Daddy was upset about he's all right now.'

'I'm not that naïve. This is your dogged reporter you're talking to, you know, I wasn't born yesterday. You've been going out with Falcone what——? One, two weeks? And your father has been back at work a week. Quite a coincidence, that.'

Farrah licked her lips nervously. 'There's nothing coincidental about it. Daddy's better, that's all.'

Nigel shook his head. 'That isn't true. I know your father felt pretty sick after your mother died, but not that ill. It's been over six weeks now, and I know there's more to this than you're actually telling. At a guess I would say your father was in some sort of financial difficulty.'

'That isn't true!' She slammed her glass down heavily on the table in front of her. 'My father had a large insurance policy that he cashed in as soon as he knew Mummy was ill. He wanted only the best for her.'

'And he got it,' Nigel said drily. 'How much has

Falcone given you? And for what, that's what I want
to know? Surely Falcone hasn't resorted to paying for
your services!'

'You're as bad as Dad——' she broke off as she saw
his sharpened look. 'For goodness' sake, Nigel! Leave
the subject alone!'

'Because I'm too near the truth,' he scoffed.

'You're nowhere *near* the truth!'

'Oh, but I am. Your father didn't have an insurance
policy, he told me that in one of his more depressed
moods. And Falcone is deliberately feeding the
rumours about the two of you by not reporting it in
any of his own newspapers. Almost as if this thing between the two of you is serious.'

'And what if it is?' Farrah flashed.

'So you get married and live happily ever after!
Come *on*, Farrah! You have to have more sense than
to think that. There've been other women, other
affairs, and none of them meant a thing. Like you, they
probably all thought they were different, but they
weren't, and neither are you. He just enjoys the chase,
all men do,' he added almost gently.

'Stop it, Nigel!' she said between gritted teeth. 'I've
had so many people giving me advice that I don't
need, that if one more person starts interfering I swear
I'll scream the place down.'

'All right, all right, subject closed. But I would just
like to know——'

'Subject closed, Nigel,' she told him firmly. 'I want
to hear about your work. What are you working on at
the moment?'

'Ah, now that's another interesting subject. I'm
afraid it involves mentioning Falcone again,' he warned
her.

'It does? Okay,' she sighed. 'Go ahead.'

Whatever she talked about—or to whom—it always

came back to the same subject, Joel Falcone. And yet two weeks ago she hadn't even seen him, let alone talked to him. He seemed to fill her whole life now, and although she didn't like to admit it, she missed him. And he had only left today! She had another week to get through, and then she still didn't know if she would see him. He changed so rapidly, from the cold aloof stranger to the man straining her to him with passionate intensity, that she found all thoughts of him confused when she wasn't actually with him. And then she was a trembling mass of expectation, of what she wasn't sure.

'I'm being sent out to the States, supposedly because the extra experience will be good for my career.'

'Supposedly?'

'Mmm. It's too sudden, Farrah. I only found out today, and I leave early next week.'

'Early next week! But that only gives you a few days.'

'Exactly, so you see this is in the nature of a good-bye. It's too convenient, Farrah. Oh, not for me,' he gave a wry smile, 'but for a certain person I'm not allowed to mention.'

'Joel?' Her eyes were wide with shock. She shook her head. 'I'm sure you're wrong. Joel wouldn't——'

'Oh, wouldn't he? You're the one that's wrong. Joel Falcone is behind this move, all right. I'm just wondering why he considers me a threat. I mean, I'm not that important, am I? We only dated a few months.'

Farrah had the grace to look guilty. 'That's my fault, I'm afraid,' she told him softly. 'I told Joel—I told him I was in love with you.'

'You did! But—Oh, I get it, the jealousy routine. Well, if it's any consolation to you, it worked. I'm now to be removed out of harm's way. I take back all that I said earlier, the poor man must be besotted with you.'

'That's the one thing he isn't. I don't understand how he found out who you are, I only called you Nigel, no surname was mentioned.'

'Men like Falcone can find these things out by a few telephone calls. And his every wish is someone's else's command. Not that I mind going to the States, you understand. It'll be great experience and it could have taken me a long time to get there on my own steam. It's just the way it's being done that annoys me.'

'Well, I knew nothing about it, absolutely nothing.'

Nigel chuckled. 'Oh, I believe you. Falcone is hardly likely to tell you he's removing the competition, that would defeat the object. No, I think he imagined I would be gone before you had a chance to see me again. I almost did, actually. I was so annoyed I wasn't going to bother to see you again, but then I thought, why should I be annoyed because you love the guy? You can't force love, and if he's the one for you then it's none of my business.'

She squeezed his hand gratefully, relieved that at last someone accepted the way she felt without passing judgment on her. 'Thanks, Nigel. And I'm sorry, Joel had no right to do what he's done.'

'Like I said, I don't mind. I just thought you should know to what lengths he'll go to to keep you.'

It was late when she got back to the flat, but to her surprise her father was still sitting in the lounge. This was somewhat unusual to start with, as he usually only stayed awake long enough to make sure she was home safely. Something was wrong, very wrong. It was there in the rigid set of his shoulders and the anger in the green eyes so like her own.

'Something wrong, Daddy?' She sat on the hearthrug at his feet.

'You could say that,' his answer was controlled. 'Beth called this evening while you were out.'

Farrah's eyes dropped. 'Did she?'

'Mmm. She wanted to know if you would like to go up tomorrow for the night.' Still that even tone.

'I see.' She licked her suddenly dry lips.

Her father shot up out of his chair and Farrah though she had never seen such a look of anger on his face. 'Do you see, Farrah?' he burst out. 'Do you see how humiliated I felt when I expressed my surprise at you going to Beth's two weekends in a row, and she denied all knowledge of seeing you last weekend. Do you *see* that!'

She stood up, her look beseeching. 'Oh, Daddy, please try to understand.'

'Oh, I understand. You lied to me. You went away with Falcone last weekend, didn't you?'

'I—well—yes, I did! But it isn't what it seems.'

'Isn't what it seems! God, Farrah, I thought your mother and I had brought you up better than this. To go away for the weekend with a man you hardly know is bad enough, without lying about it too. At least have the courage to admit it.'

'I didn't want to hurt you,' she said brokenly, her eyes pleading for his understanding.

'And you think I'm not hurt now! Oh, Farrah,' he shook his head. 'To go behind my back in this underhand way!'

'And if I'd told you, Daddy? What then? More recriminations like these? I had to go, I wish you'd understand that.'

'You had to go!' He was really angry now. 'Are you so infatuated with the man that you couldn't wait to go off with him behind my back? To so betray my trust in you!'

'Oh, Daddy, *please*——'

'No, Farrah, this thing has gone too far. At first I thought it best to let you have your head, give you the freedom to get him out of your system in your own

time. But this—this *affair* has to stop now. A man like
Joel Falcone will only use you and discard you. I
would rather you finished with him now before he
humiliates you beyond healing.'

'I can't do that,' she shook her head. 'It's impossible.'

'Is he such a good lover that you can't leave him? I
can't believe you actually love the man. He's cold and
ruthless, and he'll only ever hurt you.'

'Like you're doing?' she choked over the words.
'You're too late with all this advice. I love him, you see.
I think I did from the moment I first met him.' And
she knew it was irrevocably true. She loved Joel, loved
him enough to wish that none of this was pretence,
that he really did love her enough to drop Laura Bennett for her. But he didn't. He found her physically
attractive, and perhaps that was enough for now, but
she knew that eventually she would want more than
that, that she would want his love too.

'Oh God!' Her father dropped tiredly into an armchair. 'How can you, Farrah? How can you!'

She moved to kneel before him, taking his hands
away from his downbent head and holding them
tightly between her own. 'It just happened, Daddy.
Look, you know how it was with you and Mummy,
how you fell in love with each other at first sight?
Well, it was like that with me. I tried to fight it, I know
his reputation, but it makes no difference. I love him.'

'Good God!' her father groaned. 'He ought to be
ashamed of himself. And I told him so too.'

'You—you told him?' Her brow creased in puzzle-
ment. 'When did you see him?'

'I didn't.' He pushed back his grey-streaked brown
hair. 'He telephoned this evening too.'

Farrah sat back on her heels. 'He *telephoned*? *Tonight*?

'Yes. I suppose I should have told you earlier, but I

was so angry about Beth's call that I just lost my temper.'

'Er—what did he want?' She tried to sound casual, but there was an eagerness in her voice that she couldn't disguise.

'To speak to you, of course, child,' he answered impatiently.

'And did you—did you tell him that I was out with Nigel?' She waited with bated breath for his answer.

'Well, he asked, so I told him,' her father admitted guiltily.

'Oh, Daddy!' Huge tears gathered in her eyes. Almost the last thing Joel had said to her was that she wasn't to see Nigel again. What on earth must he think of her? More to the point, what had her father said to him?

'And I gave him a piece of my mind,' he further admitted.

She sighed resignedly. 'What did you say to him?'

'Only that he ought to know better than to be carrying on an affair with a teenager, that I found the whole thing disgusting, and I wanted him to stop seeing you.'

'And his reply?' Her eyes were full of apprehension.

'He politely but firmly told me to mind my own business. I must say, I expected something stronger from him.'

'And his reaction to my being out with Nigel?' She felt that the answer to this question would be more important.

'Chilling silence,' came the quick response. 'He rang off straight after that, without actually stating his reason for calling you in the first place.'

Farrah stood up. 'I don't think that really matters now, Joel won't call back.'

Her father looked at her closely. 'Because of Nigel?'

'He didn't want me to see him again, in fact, he

made a point of asking me not to.'

'Then why did you, if he made such a thing about it?'

She began to pace up and down the room. 'I did it because I was hurt, out of spite, I suppose. But I never actually thought Joel would find out. That sounds rather silly in the circumstances, but it's true. I met Nigel out of childish pique and regretted it immediately. I'd just learnt from you that Joel left today, and not yesterday as I thought, and I suppose I was jealous. But when I was out I realised I didn't have any right to be, if Joel chose to say goodbye to me yesterday that's his affair. I don't have any right to object.'

'Then you should have if he can dictate your friends. It should work both ways, Farrah.'

She smiled wanly. 'Not with someone like Joel.'

'Then you're well out of it. Nigel's more your type, you should stick to him.'

'Too late, Daddy, Nigel's going to America early next week.'

'And you don't think Falcone will call you again?'

'I'm sure of it.'

Her father stood up, putting an arm about her shoulders. 'Then I'm glad. I realise you don't feel the same way at the moment, but you will. Just give it a little time.'

'More than a little, I'm afraid,' she said dejectedly.

'I'm sorry, Farrah,' he looked at her closely. 'Maybe if I'd realised how much you love him . . .'

'You would still have acted the same,' she told him. 'You're trying to protect me, I realise that.'

She lay awake a long time that night, her thoughts all of Joel. Would she see him again? Their relationship had gone past pretence now, and Joel would genuinely not like her having seen Nigel. And yet why had Joel parted from her yesterday, who had he seen yesterday evening, the eve of his departure? There were so many questions she wanted answering and no one to answer them.

Why had Joel called her all the way from America? It must have been very important for him to go to all that trouble. Her thoughts plagued her long into the night, and she found it difficult to even think about sleep. *Would* she ever see Joel again? She had told her father, firmly, no. And yet couldn't Joel be cruel enough to make her go through with their bargain, and be all the more determined because she had defied him? Oh God, she hoped so! To see him was all she asked.

No matter how she tried she couldn't wipe out the memory of their last meeting, of the way he had kissed and caressed her to fever pitch, until she had thought he would make love to her there and then. And she would have let him! None of her past inhibitions seemed important when she was with him, and she had no thought of denial when she was in his arms.

Joel didn't deserve to live his life through without love, without the warmth and passion of a woman who loved him above others. And she was that woman! Well, a girl really, but in the strength of his arms she became a woman, a woman who more than equalled his passion, if not experience.

Joel wanted her, he admitted as much, and she could tell his desire for her at his slightest touch. Would it be enough? Could she let herself be taken, and then later discarded? Did she love him enough to let it be so, or could it be that she loved him too little to let such a thing happen? She didn't know! Oh God, what could she do, trapped between her love for him and the desire she could not deny, or even wanted to.

She turned over with a groan. The clock said two o'clock, and she hadn't had any sleep at all. It could be days before Joel returned, he had been unsure of the length of his stay, and she hadn't liked to press him. Was every night he was away to be spent in passionate longing for him, in this sleepless void that caused her only agony of mind and body?

Seconds, minutes, or could it have been hours later, the telephone began ringing, and kept ringing until Farrah dragged herself out of the restless sleep she had fallen into, where a bell kept ringing and ringing, until it became a reality. Her movements were slow and sluggish, and it took her quite a few minutes to get her thoughts together enough to put on her wrap and go out into the hallway where the telephone was situated.

Her father was there before her, and she looked at him through sleepy eyes as he lifted the receiver. Within seconds he was handing the receiver over to her, his expression weary. 'Doesn't the damn man realise it's five o'clock in the morning!' He walked away shaking his head, his bedroom door closing quietly behind him.

Farrah raised the telephone to her ear with a shaking hand. 'Yes?' she asked breathlessly.

'Farrah?' came the terse reply.

Joel! Oh God, it was Joel! But who else would it have been, only he was arrogant enough to telephone at this time of the morning. 'Do you realise what the time is?' she asked stupidly.

'Of course I damn well do!' he snapped back, his voice so clear it almost sounded as if he were in the next room. If only he were! 'I spoke to your father earlier.'

'I know.'

'Then you also know he told me of your meeting with Nigel? God, Farrah, I only went out of the country today!'

'I know, Joel, at least I do now. Why did you say

goodbye to me yesterday?' It was a question that had
bothered her all evening, and she had to know the
answer, no matter how angry it made him.

'I didn't call you to answer damn fool questions!'
he answered impatiently.

'By why, Joel? Why! Just answer me that.'

'All right. *All right!* I said goodbye to you yesterday because I didn't want to see you again before I
left.'

'I see.' She bit her lip at his callousness.

'Do you? I doubt it. You can't begin to understand
my feelings in anything. Were you so desperate for
male company that you accepted this Nigel's invitation
as soon as my back was turned? Or was it already
arranged between the two of you and I conveniently
left you to it?'

There could be no doubt in her mind that Joel was
furiously angry with her. And yet why should *he* be
any more angry than she! 'You have no right to say
such things. I told you Nigel had finished with me. I
didn't lie.'

'You said *he* had finished with *you*, but obviously
you didn't feel the same way. What a little fraud you
are, Farrah. And I said they were unawakened eyes!' he
said in disgust.

'What are you saying now? That I lied to you about
that too?'

'Why not? The first day I saw you I thought your
innocence too good to be true. Those eyes of yours lie,
Farrah, and you lied too. You couldn't wait for me
to leave before getting in touch with your past lover,
could you? I should have taken you when I had the
chance! And I had the chance so many times, didn't
I?' he taunted sneeringly. 'Your protestations were
mere words of denial while your body said otherwise.

You're just like all women, Farrah, you can't be without a man for long.'

'Oh God, Joel, what are you saying to me?' Her
eyes were wide with horror.

'That you're nothing but a slut, like Laura, like all
goddamned women! Nothing less than a common
little——'

'Do you honestly believe that?' she cut in, her voice
shaking with emotion.

'Oh, I believe it. I rarely say things I don't mean.'

Her answer was to slowly put down the receiver and
go back to her bedroom. That Joel should say such
things to her, that he should *believe* such things. How
could he! She threw herself down on the bed, her body
racked by deep sobs. To say such things! That she
was a slut, and to liken her to Laura whom he despised
almost to hatred. Oh, how could she bear it? How
could she bear it!

Her sobs finally ceased and she fell asleep again, her
cheeks tear-wet and her eyes red-rimmed from crying so
much. And that was how her father found her an hour
later when he came to wake her. Still dressed in her
wrap, and draped across the coverlet of her bed, she lay
with her cheek cradled into her hand like a baby, and
Paul Halliday felt a burning anger towards Joel Falcone. What was the man doing to his little girl to make
her so unhappy, the callous devil?

He shook her shoulder gently. 'Farrah? Come on,
baby, wake up!'

Her eyes felt sore as she opened them, and she felt
cold from her lack of clothing. 'Wh—what it is,
Daddy? Is something wrong?'

Her father sighed. 'He's on the telephone again,
baby. He wants to talk to you.'

Farrah was fully awake now. She pushed back the
hair from her forehead, blinking rapidly. 'I don't want

to speak to him,' she said dully.

'He was afraid of that. He says you put the telephone down on him the last time.'

'I did. What else did he say?'

'Only that he *has* to speak to you.'

She shook her head. 'Tell him no, Daddy. I won't talk to him.'

Her father stood up. 'He isn't going to like it.'

'I couldn't give a damn what he likes!' she flared. 'I don't want any more to do with him.'

'Okay, I'll tell him.'

Within seconds he was back again. 'He's very insistent, Farrah,' he told her. 'He won't be put off. I think you should just talk to him.'

Farrah shook her head again. 'No, thanks, Daddy. Not just so that he can hurl verbal abuse at me again.'

'Is that what he did? My God, he's got a nerve!'

She smiled wanly. 'He thinks he has good reason. Just tell him that I won't speak to him.'

'Is that your final word?'

'No, my final word is to tell him to go to hell! I'm sorry, but that's the way I feel.'

She was back in bed, the covers pulled firmly over her, when her father came back. She looked at him enquiringly. 'He hung up,' he confirmed. 'And he said to tell you he's half way to hell already. And I guess he is, I'm sure he's been drinking.'

CHAPTER TEN

'IT'S for you, Farrah,' Fiona held out the telephone receiver to her. 'Mr Falcone again.'

Farrah shook her head. 'Tell him I'm out of the office.'

Fiona sighed. 'I told him that this morning. I don't think he'll believe me a second time, in fact, I don't think he believed me the first time.'

'Tell him anything you like, then. I don't want to talk to him.' She turned away.

'I gathered that,' Fiona replied dryly. 'Okay, if that's the way you feel.'

'It is,' Farrah said firmly.

'All right. Mr Falcone?' she spoke into the receiver. 'Farrah isn't here at the moment, can I take a message?' A slight pause while she pointedly ignored Farrah's frantic shaking of her head. 'Fiona Mason,' she supplied. 'That's right. Yes, Mr Falcone, I quite understand. I'll tell her.'

'Well,' she turned to Farrah once she had rung off, 'aren't you interested in what he had to say?'

'Not particularly,' Farrah lied.

'Oh, then I won't bother to tell you,' Fiona said casually.

'Don't tease, Fiona.' Her hands trembled. 'Tell me!'

'I don't see why you couldn't have spoken to him yourself. All right, all right, I gather you have your reasons. He told me to tell you he's sorry, for what he didn't say, but I think you know.'

Farrah's eyes widened. 'He said he was *sorry*?'

'Mmm. It must have been some argument for him to keep phoning you like this. That's the fourth call in three days.'

'He telephoned twice on Saturday and once on Sunday too,' she admitted ruefully. 'And it wasn't exactly an argument, more a lack of trust on his part.'

'Well, surely you can see for yourself that he's regretting whatever happened. You can't go on punishing a man of his type for ever, he'll just find someone else.'

'Maybe that wouldn't be such a bad thing,' Farrah said slowly. 'For both of us.'

Fiona shook her head. 'Not for you, and certainly not for him. You've been walking about like a ghost all week, and he must be spending a fortune on telephone calls. Oh, I know he can afford it, but that isn't the point. It must be very humiliating for him when you won't even speak to him.'

'I *can't* talk to him, Fiona. If you could have heard what he said to me!'

'I can imagine that when he loses his temper he isn't too particular what he says. You have to accept that with a man of his temperament. You should at least speak to him, hear what he has to say.'

'Maybe,' she agreed. 'Maybe next time he calls.'

She knew there was no maybe about it, the next time he called she *would* speak to him. It had been pure agony denying herself the chance to talk to him, but his last words had hurt her so much that she couldn't bear it if he continued to insult her. She had been wrong to go out with Nigel, she knew that, but she hadn't expected Joel to react so violently.

Her decision had been made in vain. Two days now and Joel had not called again. Every time the telephone rang she expected it to be him, but it never was. And she was missing him unbearably. For almost a week he had been gone, and every day seemed like a week. When would he be home? and would he inform her of

his return when he did? She very much doubted it. As
Fiona had said, a man like Joel would soon find someone else if thwarted too much. But what of their bargain? She had no doubt he would still keep her to
that, no matter what his own feelings were in the
matter.

Her heart sank and her mouth went dry as she saw
the woman just entering the building. The other girls
had gone out for their Friday lunch-time meal, and as
she wasn't very good company at the moment she had
decided not to inflict her company on them, going out
to lunch on her own. And now here was Laura Bennett, the other owner of this very prosperous firm,
walking into the Falcone building as Farrah was walking out. And there could be no doubt that the other
woman had seen and recognised her by the sharpen-
ing of those green cat-like eyes. Farrah would have
turned and walked away, but Laura Bennett seemed to
be walking purposefully towards her and escape was
impossible.

As the last time she had seen her, Laura Bennett
was perfectly attired, dressed in a tailored cream skirt
and jacket, contrasted with a black fitted blouse. Her
long black hair was brushed away down her back,
shiny as a raven's wing, and her make-up perfect to the
last detail.

Farrah, in contrast, felt perfectly drab. She had on
her usual denims and matching denim waistcoat with
a checked shirt beneath. Her hair was its usual riot
of waves, and the only colour to her face came from
her huge green eyes surrounded by thick dark lashes.
Nevertheless, she faced the other woman with a steady
gaze, not showing her nervousness by the flicker of an
eyelash.

'Miss Halliday,' Laura Bennett's voice came out as
a purr, not at all like her harsh tone of their last meet-

ing. 'It *is* Miss Halliday, isn't it?'

This woman made Farrah feel extra tall, and in spite of her own slenderness, rather large. The actress was so small and dainty, and her beauty unmarred, and Farrah wondered at Joel's indifference to such a woman. 'Yes,' she answered rather shyly, wishing they could move away from the Falcone building where they might be recognised. The gossip had died down a little in Joel's absence, and all that it needed to re-ignite it was the sighting of herself and Laura Bennett talking together.

'Are you going to lunch?' the actress asked.

'Well, I was, yes.'

'Good,' Laura Bennett smiled at her. 'Perhaps I can join you for coffee or something?'

Farrah's eyes widened. 'J-join me?'

'Why not?' We're two adults, surely we can act as such?'

Farrah wasn't so sure about that, she had seen the other woman's temper the last time they met. 'I guess so,' she said reluctantly. 'But I was only going to the local café. It isn't very smart, I'm afraid.' She didn't understand this woman's behaviour, but she felt sure her manner owed nothing to friendliness. Goodness, she had looked ready to scratch her eyes out last Saturday!

Laura Bennett led the way over to a low green sports car parked precariously on the forecourt. 'I think we can do a little better than that,' she said smoothly.

Farrah drew back. 'I don't think so. I only have an hour for lunch.'

'Don't worry,' Laura flicked open the passenger door before walking round to slide in behind the wheel. She looked up at Farrah as she still stood outside the car. 'You'll be back within the hour.'

'I don't see the need for this,' Farrah denied. 'We

can't have anything to talk about, Miss Bennett.'

Laura Bennett gave a tinkling laugh, flicking back her long hair as she turned on the ignition. 'I think you underestimate the situation, Miss Halliday. Although Joel may have made our friendship seem casual I can assure you I don't regard it as such. Now would you get in the car?'

'I don't think——'

'Get in!' Laura Bennett's voice hardened to anger.

Farrah did as she was told, recognising a force of character to equal Joel's. The other woman didn't seem in a hurry to start their conversation, and Farrah was no more eager, and consequently the short drive to one of the rather well-known restaurants in town was accomplished in complete silence, a rather uneasy silence on Farrah's part, but the other woman seemed very relaxed and self-assured.

The waiter saw them seated and had served them with plates of smoked salmon before Laura Bennett spoke again. 'How long have you known Joel?' she asked casually.

Farrah knew there was nothing casual about it, and she wished she had had the strength of character to refuse to come with this woman who could only ever feel dislike for her. 'I've worked at Falcone's for three years,' she answered evasively.

The other woman nibbled delicately at a piece of smoked salmon. 'That doesn't exactly answer my question, now does it?'

'Maybe not,' Farrah said sullenly.

'So?'

'So I don't think it's me you should be talking to. Joel would be able to answer your questions so much better than I.' Farrah herself ignored the food, wishing only to escape.

'Oh, I've already spoken to Joel, a very enlightening conversation,' she said with satisfaction.

'You—you've spoken to Joel?' She couldn't help her surprise. But why should she be? These two had been friends a long time, they were business partners, and that gave them an intimacy that excluded others.

'Mmm. He called me from America. He called you too, I gather? A pity he couldn't have told you then.' But she didn't look very sorry about it. 'Joel wanted to tell you himself, of course, but found it impossible to do.'

'Found what impossible?' Farrah asked with a feeling of dread.

'I'd really rather not be the one to tell you this, but you know how men are about these things. Joel realises now that things between you must end,' Laura Bennett patted delicately at her mouth with her serviette. 'Do eat something, my dear, it's delicious.'

'No, thank you,' Farrah replied stiffly. 'What did Joel want you to tell me, Miss Bennett?'

'Only that he realises he made a mistake by getting involved with you. I think you should know that the two of us intend getting married as soon as he returns, in fact I would say our relationship is already back on its normal footing.'

On the eve of his departure, Joel had been with this woman! No wonder he didn't want to see Farrah that evening, he had already been heavily engaged. And yet somehow this didn't ring true. Joel wasn't the type of man to send Laura Bennett to tell her he had changed his mind about their pretence. He might be ruthless and arrogant, but he had never been deliberately cruel where she was concerned.

No, something was definitely wrong here. Joel's words about this woman had been no less harsh during their brief telephone conversation, he had still seemed to despise her. So what was Laura Bennett doing here?

Why bother to tell her that Joel didn't want to see her again, surely she could be expected to know that when Joel didn't call her again. And yet he hadn't! Not for two days now, and he had told Fiona to tell her he was sorry! She had thought he meant for the argument they had had, but it could just as well have been for the news this woman was so enjoying giving her. Oh God, yes, it could! Farrah's shoulders slumped.

Laura Bennett gave a satisfied smile, Farrah's thoughts blatantly transparent to her narrowed eyes. 'I hope I can count on you being sensible about this,' she carried on smoothly, pressing home her point. 'This could all be very embarrassing for Joel when he returns, now that he realises his mistake in involving you in our silly quarrel.'

'He should have thought of that earlier!' snapped Farrah. 'It wasn't my idea to go out together.'

'I'm sure it wasn't,' soothed the older woman. 'Joel's a very attractive man, I know that. He must seem very sophisticated to a young girl like you.'

Farrah looked at her sharply. This woman didn't know of their bargain, and if she didn't know that then how could she be sure she was telling her the truth about Joel?

'You must surely understand that you can't possibly go on working for Joel?'

'Are you trying to tell me that Joel wants me to leave Falcone's?'

'That's exactly what I'm saying.'

Farrah smiled. 'You must think me very naïve,' she said stiffly. 'I may not know Joel as well as you do, but I certainly know him well enough to know he wouldn't send *you* to tell me our—our——'

'Affair,' Laura Bennett put in sharply.

Farrah's eyes flashed. 'Yes, affair! Joel wouldn't end things like this. I know he wouldn't.' She now felt more confident. Whatever this woman knew about herself and Joel, she didn't know of their bargain, and if she didn't know about that then she didn't know anything.

'Joel soon tires of these little relationships with other women. We've been friends for so long, you see, and I know him so well. But this affair means nothing to Joel. Nothing! And let me tell you, we'll be back together once he returns.'

'I didn't come here to argue with you, Miss Bennett,' Farrah said calmly. 'When I hear from Joel's own lips that he doesn't want to see me any more, then maybe I'll believe it, until then I think it would be better if we both forgot this conversation ever took place.'

Laura Bennett's mouth tightened perceptibly. 'Don't get clever with me, little girl. If I tell you to leave Joel alone, then that's exactly what I want you to do. You're only the latest of many, and I'm trying to help you and save some of your pride.'

Farrah almost laughed at this. And Joel had said no one would be hurt! Well, he was right about himself and Laura, the only reason she was reacting now was through pique. But *she* was being hurt even if they weren't. 'You're trying to help yourself, Miss Bennett.' She stood up, pushing her chair back clumsily. 'Excuse me, but I don't think we have any more to say to each other.'

Two bright red spots of colour appeared on the other woman's cheeks, evidence of her blazing anger. 'I haven't finished with you yet!'

'Then I'm sorry, but I have no intention of listening to any more.' Farrah spun on her heel and made her way across the restaurant, her head held high. A waiter rushed forward to open the door for her and she walked out blindly, colliding with one of the two men just about to enter. 'Sorry,' she mumbled, the

tears in her eyes giving her only a fuzzy outline of the
two men.

Someone grasped her arm. 'Farrah!'

She blinked rapidly, partly dispersing the unshed
tears and at last being able to see who was speaking to
her. 'Simon!' she sighed her relief.

His eyes narrowed at her pale face. 'Are you all right,
Farrah?'

She moved out of his grasp. 'Yes—yes, I'm fine.' She
glanced frantically behind her, fervently hoping
Laura Bennett hadn't decided to follow her out of the
restaurant. 'I was just leaving,' she added, when no
sign could be seen of the other woman.

'Why don't you join us for a coffee?' he persisted.

'No—no, I don't think so.' Another look behind her.
'I have to be going now, I'll be late back from lunch.'

Simon grinned. 'I'm sure Joel won't complain,' he
teased.

The man with him looked at her with renewed interest. 'Farrah?' he said slowly. 'Farrah Halliday!' he exclaimed. 'You're Joel's latest, aren't you?'

Her eyes darkened with pain. Yes, she thought
wearily, she was Joel's latest. God, how casual that
sounded when she *loved* him!

Simon glared at his companion. 'Damn it, Harry,
do you have to be so tactless?'

'It's all right,' Farrah touched his arm. 'But I must
be going now.' She had the dreadful feeling that at
any moment now Laura Bennett was going to come
out of the restaurant and give Simon something else
to write about in the newspapers. And that she didn't
want, especially in Joel's absence. 'Nice seeing you
again, Simon.' She smiled her goodbye to Harry.

'I'll take a rain-check on that lunch, Harry,' was
Simon's parting shot as he quickly followed Farrah,
catching her up quite a way along the street. 'Hey, slow

down, I'm not as young as you are!'

Farrah smiled at him. 'I really do have to get back. And Joel won't excuse me anything, he's away at the moment.'

Simon nodded. 'In the States, yes, I know.'

'Of course, you're good friends, aren't you? But not good enough, apparently.'

He frowned. 'What do you mean?'

'The newspaper article. Just because I'm talking to you it doesn't mean I'm not angry.'

He looked puzzled. 'You were *angry* about it?'

'I still am. It's caused me a lot of embarrassment.' She didn't slacken her speed. She only had about ten minutes of her lunch hour left and there was still quite a way to go to the office block.

'Didn't you know about the article?'

'Joel did say it was a possibility,' she admitted. 'But as you're his friend I would have thought you could have curbed your eagerness for a juicy bit of gossip out of respect for Joel's feelings.'

'Hey, hold on a minute! I asked Joel about printing that particular article. Of course, I wouldn't have published it if he'd been against it.'

'You mean you asked Joel and he approved?'

'Exactly. What was going on at that restaurant?'

'Just a minute.' She stopped him. 'You mean Joel actually encouraged you to print that story? I don't believe it!'

'Okay, don't believe it, just tell me what you and Laura were doing eating together?'

'So you can print that in your newspaper too?' She shook her head. 'Oh no!'

He looked hurt. 'Don't be like that, Farrah. I told you, I had Joel's approval.'

'So you say.'

'It's true. So why did you meet Laura?'

'I didn't. And I was not eating with her either, we met by accident as I was going to lunch and she invited herself along,' she grimaced.

'Laura was at Falcone's?'

'Mmm,' she looked round. 'And so are we. I have to go in.'

'Do you know when Joel's returning?'

Her eyes widened. 'Why should I know? Shouldn't you be asking Miss Bennett that? She seems to be the one who spoke to him last.'

'So that's it. I shouldn't believe everything she tells you. You represent quite a threat to Laura, quite a threat. You see, although they aren't married, Laura has never had her position as the future Mrs Falcone seriously questioned before.'

'Don't be ridiculous!' Farrah blushed as Fiona and the other girls from the office walked by, their interest in them obvious by the looks directed at them. 'Now look what you've done! And there's been enough gossip these last two weeks without this too. Goodbye, Simon.'

'Who was the dishy man?' Fiona asked later. 'He was quite something.'

'Don't you start!' Farrah replied crossly.

'Okay,' laughed her friend. 'But he was rather nice. You sure know how to pick them!'

Farrah gave her a scathing look. 'He's a friend of Joel's. I happened to meet him by accident when I was out at lunchtime.'

Fiona grinned. 'I believe you.'

'I should hope so!'

Farrah took her time going home that night, her father had left earlier than her this evening and would already have gone out by the time she returned. Angie had asked her to work late, and as she had nothing else to do it had seemed like a good idea to stay. Most of the other girls had dates anyway, and so it was only fair that she, who didn't have an engagement, should be the one to do the extra work. Why not? She had nothing to hurry home to, nothing and no one.

The flat seemed curiously empty in her father's absence, and after preparing herself a sandwich and a mug of coffee, she wandered into her bedroom. She hadn't stayed at home as much in the evenings as she had this past week for years. She had been out with a couple of the girls in the office to discotheques and the cinema in the weeks preceding Joel's sudden advent into her life, when she wasn't out with Nigel of course, but just lately that seemed to have faded out. The girls seemed slightly shy about talking to her any more, let alone actually inviting her to join them for an evening out.

She lifted the lid of the jewel box Joel had given her, running loving fingers over the green glittering stones and the platinum chain. Her only link with Joel, and it was a link that had to be hidden from all eyes except her own. The jewel box had remained hidden among her clothes in one of her drawers, taken out only when she was alone. She snapped the lid shut with a firm click. It was no good tormenting herself with what could never be.

She heard the telephone ringing with a feeling of relief; she needed saving from her own thoughts. The voice at the other end of the telephone was the last one in the world she had expected to hear. 'Joel!' she breathed his name softly, as if afraid to say it in case he hung up.

'Are you going to put the telephone down on me again?'

She almost choked over her relief at the lightness of his tone. 'No,' her voice broke. 'I—I want to talk to you.'

'And you believe me, about being sorry?'

'I believe you. And I'm sorry I went out with Nigel. I was angry, but I still shouldn't have done it.' She was actually talking to him! Oh, Joel, I love you!

'And were you angry today too?'

His voice had changed, but it was difficult to tell over the telephone line, with Joel thousands of miles away, what his mood was right now. 'Today?' she repeated slowly. 'What happened today?'

'You tell me.' The line crackled between them. 'You met Simon today, so I've been told.'

'Is that what he told you?' she asked angrily. 'Oh, how could he!'

'Simon didn't tell me,' he informed her calmly. 'Someone saw you leaving the restaurant with him. You aren't doing much to help our pretence, are you?'

Farrah felt her anger rising against him. 'Is that all you care about, your damned pretence? You've been away a week now and all you can do is talk about that damned stupid pretence! I met Simon as I was *leaving* that restaurant. I didn't even want to speak to him, but he wouldn't leave me alone.'

'So just what were you doing in that particular restaurant? I thought you didn't like the sort of place my friends frequented.'

'You may be sorry for what you said to me the other day, but you still don't trust me,' she accused.

'So you aren't going to tell me?'

Oh God, they were arguing again! 'No, I'm not,' she answered firmly.

'Good girl, Farrah. You're a loyal little thing, even to those who don't deserve your loyalty. And Laura is just such a person. You don't have to protect her, you know, Simon told me how you bumped into him.'

Farrah gasped. 'You mean you knew all the time I hadn't been out with him! Oh, Joel, you're so cruel! Why do you do it?'

'Lack of trust, as you said, little one.' She could almost hear the cynicism in his voice. 'But I'm learning, all the time, I'm learning.'

'So why haven't you called me?'

'Missed me?' He answered her with another question of his own.

'No!' she lied. 'Why should I?'

'Why indeed? Simon says you aren't looking too happy with life at the moment.'

'Simon says altogether too much,' came her tart reply. 'And about things that don't concern him. When did you speak to him?'

'He called me this afternoon. But not before Laura. She really enjoyed telling me that she'd seen you with Simon. I could cheerfully have wrung her neck at that moment!'

'Oh, but I——'

'Didn't meet Simon? I know that. You met Laura, by her design I have no doubt. She had a different version, and it didn't ring true. Simon seemed very concerned about you,' he added mockingly.

'So that's why you called! Well, my unhappy state has nothing to do with you, nothing at all!'

'Don't put the telephone down on me again, Farrah!' Joel warned harshly. 'Once I can forget, twice is just once too many.'

'Are you threatening me, Joel? Because if you are, I——'

'Farrah!' he snapped at her firmly. 'Just calm down. You're too quick to jump to conclusions where I'm concerned. It seems to be true of both of us. I haven't called you the last couple of days because I thought it better to let you get over your anger with me in peace and quiet. Also, I've been pretty tied up, trying to cram another week's work into forty-eight hours so that I can return to England.'

Her heart leapt. 'You're coming home?' She couldn't keep the excitement out of her voice.

'Tomorrow evening some time,' he confirmed.

'Oh, Joel! That's—that's—that will be nice,' she amended.

'I'm hoping it will be more than that, but we'll talk about that tomorrow.'

'You want me to meet you? No——' she said shakily, 'of course you don't.'

'Honey, if I knew what time I'd be arriving I'd want you there, only you. But I can't be sure of my arrival time. What I want you to do is go to my apartment and wait for me there. You'll be expected.'

'I—I will? By whom?'

He gave a throaty chuckle. 'An American edition of George. Soames is as much the correct English butler as an American can be. I'll make sure he expects you tomorrow evening.' He went on to give her detailed directions on how to get there.

'Will you be late? What time should I go to your apartment?' She would be there at daybreak if necessary. All she wanted was to see Joel again, to perhaps be held in his arms, even if only in pretence.

'I'm hoping to arrive on the seven o'clock flight, so I should be at the apartment for eight o'clock at the latest. Seven-thirty should be time enough.'

'All right.' She had to wait all that time! It would seem like years.

'I'll have to go now, honey. You'll be there to-morrow?'

Try and keep her away! 'I'll be there,' she promised.

She dressed the next evening with more than her usual care; she wanted Joel to think her attractive. It was so important to her that she must have changed at least ten times. Clothes were strewn all over her bedroom, and she still wasn't satisfied with the result. She wanted to look sophisticated and alluring, to attract Joel to her again as he undoubtedly had been before leaving for America.

None of her clothes seemed right, and she sat down dejectedly. She had even been out this afternoon and bought two new dresses, and yet when she had returned home and fitted them on again she decided she didn't like either of them. The black flower print made her look like a schoolgirl, which she certainly didn't feel like in Joel's company, and the emerald green dress that matched her eyes was altogether too revealing for a casual evening spent at his apartment.

As his apartment! She would be completely alone with him—except for the respectable Soames—and she hadn't forgotten where their 'conversation' had left off. Her cheeks flamed. Oh no, she hadn't forgotten at all! And she hoped he hadn't either. Oh God, was it bad to think this way? If it was there was nothing she could do about it. She loved Joel, it was as simple as that.

She still wasn't satisfied with her final choice, but time was passing and already it was almost seven o'clock. The pink and black flower-print skirt and black blouse weren't exactly what she had in mind when thinking of dazzling Joel, but at least they suited her, emphasising her slender body and fair colouring.

She finally dashed out of her bedroom at seven-fifteen, still holding her hands outstretched as she waited for her nail varnish to dry properly. Her father sat in front of the television, looking up with a smile as she moved about the room putting things into her handbag.

'So you're going, are you?' he quirked an eyebrow.

Farrah sighed. 'I already told you I was.'

'I've been thinking things over, love,' he stood up,

'and if this is what you want then I'm not going to offer
any more objections. I can't interfere in your life any
more. I believe you love him, and that's enough for
me.'

She gave him a hug, kissing his cheek lovingly. 'I
love you, Daddy!'

He squeezed her hands. 'I know you do, love, but you
love Joel Falcone too. Off you go and see him.'

'Thank you, Daddy.'

She looked up at the tall building, apprehensive
about actually going up to the penthouse apartment. It
wasn't eight o'clock yet, so the chances were that Joel
hadn't arrived. What would Soames think of her?
More to the point, what had Joel told him about her,
that is, if Joel considered he had to tell his butler anything at all. She was later than her stated time, but
she blamed this on her inability to locate a taxi; there
was never one about when you really needed one.

After assuring the man at the desk that she was expected she was allowed to go up in the lift to the penthouse apartment. The receptionist would undoubtedly
call straight up to the apartment anyway, to say she
was on her way. The lift doors opened straight into a
reception room, a room such as she had never seen before. Leather armchairs, a deep-pile carpet and genuine
antiques placed at strategic points about the room all
added up to the same luxury Joel surrounded himself
with at his country home.

She looked up uncertainly as a door opened on the
far side of the room, and a man came across the carpet
towards her. The soft golden glow that illuminated
the room didn't allow for perfect vision, but it en-
abled her to see that this man was much younger than
her imaginings, he couldn't be more than thirty, and
he probably wasn't even that old.

She waited expectantly as he approached her. There

was something vaguely familiar about him, but she didn't know what it was. And he didn't act like any manservant she had ever seen before! He was carrying a tumbler half full of whisky—at least, it looked like whisky.

He raised a dark enquiring eyebrow at her, his eyes totally assessing as he looked her up and down. He obviously liked what he saw because he was smiling by the time those laughing blue eyes met hers, and the familiarity Farrah had thought she detected had disappeared completely.

'What can I do for you?' His voice was deep and attractive, and much more of a drawl than Joel's.

'I—er—I came to see Joel.'

The man gave a mocking smile, sipping casually at the whisky. Looking at him closer she thought he didn't *look* much like a manservant either, dressed in a well-fitting navy suit and a lighter blue shirt opened casually at the neck, and his hair grew low over his collar. 'Didn't we all?' he drawled.

'I—he isn't here?' Really! This man was so annoying. She was surprised at Joel employing such a man. He didn't act like an employee at all, dressed as he was and drinking Joel's whisky as if he did it every day of his life. Perhaps he did! Surely Joel couldn't know how he behaved in his absence? And the way he looked at her! So insolent.

'No, he isn't here. Why don't you come in and talk to me instead?'

'When are you expecting Joel?' she asked stiffly. The familiarity of the man!

'Any time now. But I don't think he's expecting *you.*'

Her eyes widened. 'You don't? But I——'

'You could find it very embarrassing being here when he arrives,' he interrupted her.

'I could?' she repeated stupidly.

'Very,' he agreed, smiling. 'Joel's lady-love is coming here tonight, and she's likely to scratch your eyes out.'

Laura! It had to be her. How could Joel be this cruel to her! He had had all day to let her know she wasn't wanted here tonight. He would be here in a moment, and Laura was sure to be with him. She had to get out of here before they arrived. She was shaking all over and her hands were perspiring with nervousness. She couldn't stand another encounter with Laura Bennett, especially in front of Joel.

'I—er—I have to go now. If you aren't expecting Joel I may as well leave.'

'Hey!' He moved towards her, a tall man, lean and attractive in a rakish sort of way. 'I didn't say I wasn't expecting him, I said I thought he might be otherwise engaged. You don't have to leave, at least, not alone. Will I do as a substitute? I know I'm not quite up to Joel's standard, but I'm a pretty fair replica.'

Farrah was outraged. 'How dare you? Just what do you think I am!'

'It's what you're not that's important.'

'What do you mean?'

'Like I told you, Joel's lady-love will be here any moment now. And that *isn't* you.'

'I'm leaving!' she said firmly.

'Alone?'

'Of course, alone! I don't know what sort of employee you are, but I'm sure Joel doesn't know of your behaviour. Personally, I find you very rude.'

'I'm not an employee.'

'Don't lie on top of everything else! You brazenly stand there drinking your employer's whisky, walking about the place as if you own it! Joel would sack you if he could see you now.'

He gave a deep laugh, putting down his glass and

moving towards her. Farrah backed away, not liking the devilish glint she could see in those determined blue eyes. 'Joel wouldn't sack me, honey,' he said softly. 'Even if I did work for him, which I don't.'

'Then who are you?' she asked shrilly. 'Leave me alone! Don't come any nearer!'

Her words had no effect and he only advanced further, pinning her to the wall with the look in his eyes. 'Don't be so angry, honey. I could be just as nice to you as Joel.'

'Stop it!' she said breathlessly, pushing him away. God, this was a nightmare! 'Just leave me alone!'

'What the hell is going on here?' A deep familiar voice rang out around the room. Joel! Farrah looked at him thankfully, but the harshness of his face did nothing to encourage her. 'Richie, what are you doing here?' he demanded of the man at her side.

Farrah looked at the two of them in horror. This was *Richie*, Joel's *brother*? Oh no!

CHAPTER ELEVEN

RICHIE shrugged, and now Farrah knew why he had seemed so familiar. He had a definite look of Joel about his lean muscular frame, dark hair and deep blue eyes. Not as handsome as Joel, but an attractive man in his own right. But how could she have been expected to know who he was? She had naturally assumed him to be Soames, and he hadn't offered any other explanation.

Now he grinned at his older brother. 'I came to see you.'

Joel moved further into the room, throwing his brief-case into one of the armchairs. 'You came to see *me*?' he repeated. 'I only spoke to you yesterday.'

'And what a conversation! I had to see this paragon for myself.'

Joel's mouth twisted with wry humour. 'Is that why you were attacking her when I came in?' he quirked a mocking eyebrow.

Richie's mouth dropped, and he looked at Farrah with open amazement. '*This* is Farrah?' he queried disbelievingly. 'But I thought—well, I thought——'

'Yes? Just what did you think? That Farrah would be like Laura?' Joel's amusement was evident as he helped himself to a liberal amount of whisky. He was dressed quite casually in black trousers, a black shirt, and a cream jacket fitted tautly across his shoulders.

His words reminded Farrah of Laura's imminent arrival, not that Joel seemed particularly concerned. For all the notice he was taking of her she might just as well not be here. 'I—I think I should be going now.' She made a move towards the lift doors, but Joel was quicker than her, blocking her exit quite effectively.

'Not you, Farrah,' he said deeply, the look in his eyes demanding that she stay. 'Richie's the one who's leaving.'

'Oh, but——' she began.

'Richie!' Joel said hardly.

Farrah's eyes darkened with the effort it cost her to say the next words. 'But Miss Bennett! She should be here any moment. I can't meet her again, I just can't!'

Joel looked from Richie to Farrah and then back to his brother again. 'What have you been saying now?' he asked with a sigh.

Richie shook his dark head. 'I haven't mentioned Laura. What would I have to say about her?'

'You tell me. Farrah?'

She looked from one to the other of them blankly. 'Your brother said Laura was coming here.'

Richie looked puzzled. '*I* did? I don't even remember mentioning her. I try not to think of her at all. I—wait a minute! You thought I meant *Laura*?' he grinned. 'Far from it!'

'Thought you meant Laura in what?' Joel watched them through narrowed eyes.

'I knew you were expecting Farrah. The only trouble was, I didn't realise Farrah *was* Farrah, if you know what I mean.'

'I see. Well, she's here, you've settled your curiosity about her so now you can leave.'

'I could just have come here to see you.'

Joel gave a mocking grin. 'But you didn't.'

'Okay,' his brother grinned back, 'I'm going now. I know when I'm not wanted. Nice to have met you, Farrah. Give me time and you might even come to like me too. I'm sorry about the mistake earlier, I didn't realise who you were.'

She accepted his apology with a vague smile, her

thoughts too chaotic for her to answer him sensibly. Richie had called *her* Joel's lady-love! What did it mean? Surely Joel wouldn't have told his own brother that she was truly his girl-friend. It didn't ring true, Joel had no need to go to the extreme of lying to his own family, especially as Laura didn't seem to be too popular in that direction. And yet what other explanation was there? The answer wasn't acceptable to her—well, it was acceptable, but slightly unbelievable.

'Goodbye, Richie,' Joel said firmly.

The lift doors closed with a swish and a curious silence settled over the room. Joel turned as a man entered the room. 'Good evening, Soames.'

'Mr Falcone. Will you be requiring dinner?'

'Farrah?'

'No, thank you.' She couldn't eat a thing. She felt as if she were waiting for something, and the suspense was killing her. Joel hadn't even said hello to her properly yet!

'I ate on the plane, thanks, Soames,' Joel dismissed. 'Although I could do with a pot of coffee.'

'Coffee for two, sir?'

'Right.' Joel put down his empty whisky glass. 'Let's go through to the lounge, Farrah.'

She followed him silently, appreciating the luxury and comfort of the room they now entered. Low cream armchairs, a thick brown carpet, an ebony cocktail cabinet and the most sophisticated stereo unit Farrah had ever seen, all found full approval in her eyes. Joel dropped unceremoniously into one of the low armchairs, throwing his cream jacket carelessly on the floor.

He heaved a tired sigh as Soames brought in the tray of coffee, placing it silently on the smoked glass coffee-table before quietly leaving the room again. Farrah still stood just inside the room, fidgeting awkwardly with the strap to her shoulder bag. Why didn't

he say something to her? When he did finally speak
it wasn't what she had been expecting at all.

Joel lay back in the chair, his eyes closed. 'Pour me
some coffee, honey,' he requested softly. 'Black, plenty
of sugar.'

She handed him a cup of steaming liquid. 'Are you
not feeling well?'

He sat forward, taking a thirsty gulp of the sweet hot
liquid. 'I'm feeling fine—tired, but fine.'

'You've been working hard?' she asked softly.

'Very,' he gave a wry smile. 'I haven't slept in seventy-
two hours.'

'You must be exhausted!' she said concernedly.

'A little,' he agreed. 'But I wanted to get back to
England. The first time I was ever in a hurry to return
here. I didn't even have time to see my mother while
I was in the States, which won't please her when she
finds out I was there for a week. Richie will no doubt
tell her, he has a penchant for making mischief.'

'I noticed,' she said dryly.

'What exactly was happening when I arrived? And
for goodness' sake, sit down!'

She sat down opposite him, studying his face avidly
as if engraving his features forever in her brain. She
was hungry for the sight and feel of him. This polite
conversation was time-wasting when all she wanted was
his arms about her and the hard feel of his body
against hers. Why didn't he kiss her, carry on where
they had finished at their last meeting? And this time
she would say yes. Yes, yes, yes!

She blushed now. 'Your brother thought I was—I
was——'

'I see,' he gave a half-smile. 'He isn't very observant,
is he?'

'What do you mean?' She looked at him sharply.

'Your eyes.'

Strangely his words made her feel tearful. 'Do you have to?' she said brokenly, averting her eyes at his searching look. His reference to her innocence only put them further apart.

'Have to what?'

'Make reference to my eyes. You surely didn't invite me here to talk about my eyes?'

'No,' he shook his head. 'I have a question to put to you. The reason your father took the money, I have to know it.'

'Why?'

'It's important to me,' he said simply.

Farrah stood up, turning away from him. 'Why should it be important to you now?' she asked fiercely. 'It wasn't before! You couldn't have given a damn *why* he stole the money, you were only interested in what his mistake could give you. And it gave you *me*. On a silver platter!'

'Tell me!'

'Why should I? You've bullied me for so long, Joel, a lifetime it seems to me. I told you my father stole for a good reason. I wanted to tell you why, but you wouldn't listen to me. Why should I tell you now, just because *you* decide it's the right time for you to know?'

'It's important to me, Farrah,' he repeated quietly.

'It was imporant to me too at one time. Did you ever think of that? No, of course you didn't! Well, I'll tell you, Joel, but not because *you* want to know, but because *I* want to tell you. My mother was dying, Joel, *dying*! And my father loved her so much that nothing was too wrong or too dangerous for him to do for her. She needed expert nursing, specialised treatment, and all that costs money, money my father didn't have. So he stole it. He stole for love.' By this time the tears were streaming down her cheeks, unchecked and unnoticed. It was as if a dam had burst inside her and she couldn't stop it. 'Something you wouldn't understand,' she added brokenly.

'Oh God!' she heard him groan. 'Oh God!' he repeated.

She turned on him angrily, glaring at his bent head and clasped hands. 'Don't pretend it matters to you! The aloof Joel Falcone who doesn't allow emotion to enter his life!' And she had thought she loved him! How could she have been so stupid to have forgotten the only emotion he recognised was desire. How could she! 'A little thing like my mother's death shouldn't bother you at all!'

Joel stood up, coming determinedly towards her. His hands came up to cradle each side of her tear-wet face. 'Don't cry, Farrah. I can't bear to see you cry. Just what kind of cold devil do you take me for? If you'd explained all this in the beginning——'

She wrenched away from him. 'You would have reacted the same way. I offered then to tell you why Daddy did what he did, but you didn't want to know. You were intent only on making me suffer and finding a way of getting rid of Laura Bennett at the same time. Well, you've succeeded in part, I hope you're satisfied?'

He shook his head. 'I didn't realise, Farrah. If you'd just told me.'

'I'd still be in the same predicament. Wouldn't I?'

Joel moved away, running a hand through his dark hair. 'I don't know. God, yes, I do! *Yes*, you'd still be in the same predicament! And do you know why? Then I'll tell you. And listen carefully, Farrah, because I'm only going to say this once. I shouldn't even be saying it now, but I guess you deserve some satisfaction for the hell I've put you through with my selfishness. I love you, Farrah.'

Her head snapped back and she looked at him with

shock. His face told her nothing and she thought maybe she had misheard him. 'Wh-what did you say?' she
asked breathlessly.

'I told you I would only say it the once,' he reminded
her angrily.

'P-please, Joel. Tell me again.'

'You definitely want your pound of flesh! I love
you! I love your innocence, your beauty, and lastly,
but not least, I love your body. I love the way you
respond to me, the way your hands caress me, I just
love everything about you.'

His voice had lowered huskily and Farrah shivered
with pleasure. 'Oh Joel!' she choked. 'You can't mean
it! You said you didn't believe in love.'

'I said a lot of damn fool things that would have
been better left unsaid. But I didn't lie about that. I
didn't believe in love. It took a little tigress like you
to show me how stupid my words were. Now that you
know what an idiot I am you may as well leave. I had
no right to tell you of my feelings concerning you anyway.'

Farrah snorted with feeling. 'When have rights ever
counted between us? Did you really say you *love* me?'

His eyes darkened with anger and he moved away
impatiently. 'Just leave it, Farrah. I think you should
go now. Our bargain is at an end.'

'What are you saying to me?' Her eyes widened with
horror.

'Goodbye.'

'You can't mean that! You've just told me you love
me, you can't leave it at that.'

'What else would you suggest I do?' he snapped
harshly. 'Get down on my knees and beg that you love
me in return? I wish I could! But you seem to be forgetting one important fact, I'm not free of Laura yet.

That was the reason for our relationship in the first place.'

'Oh, Joel, I don't care! I love you. I love you! I can't believe you love me. I missed you so much when you were in America—I thought the time would never pass. And I wasn't even sure if I would see you when you returned.' Her face was glowing with excitement and love, and Joel's face softened as he looked at her.

'You can't mean what you're saying,' he denied. 'You hate me, you've always hated me. Except when I've held you in my arms, and then you've hated me afterwards.' He poured himself some more coffee, drinking it in one gulp.

Farrah rushed into his arms, holding her face up eagerly, longing for his lips to part hers with passion and love. It was unbelievable! Joel *loved* her. Joel, who had always denied such emotions, had admitted his love for her. She wanted to laugh and cry at the same time, to dance and sing, but most of all she wanted to belong to him, body and soul. She put her arms about his waist, hugging him tightly to her even though he stood stiffly in her arms.

'I love you, Joel,' she said happily. 'I love you! I don't think I've ever hated you. I've been angry and hurt, yes, but never hated.'

Joel grasped her forearms painfully, bruising her soft flesh beneath the strength of his fingers. For long aching seconds those blue eyes raked disbelievingly over her glowing face. At last he gave a groan, a deep heartfelt sigh of satisfaction. She was crushed in his arms, held savagely against him, made aware of every muscle of his body as he strained her nearer.

'Farrah!' Her name was a husky caress as he burrowed deep into her throat. 'Oh, Farrah! You should belong to me! I should be able to carry you to my bed right now and make love to you until you're senseless, aware only of me and the pleasure we would share.' He bit her earlobe, but it was a pleasurable sensation rather than a painful one. 'I think I'm going to have to do it anyway! Right or no right!'

She felt herself lifted up close against him, her face buried in his chest as she rained hot impassioned kisses on his hair-roughened skin. His shirt had been opened to the waist by her eager hands and she could smell the drugging masculine odour he exuded. The dark hairs on his chest made an enticing trail down to his navel, his stomach flat and hard with muscle.

He lowered her gently on to the top of the bed, throwing off his shirt impatiently before joining her. Her hands smoothed over his shoulders, bringing his head down to hers as their lips met in consuming passion. The buttons of her blouse were no barrier to his questing fingers and his lips took and tantalised the rosy peaks now before him in their full glory, pressing her back against the bed as she groaned her heated pleasure.

Farrah wanted the pleasure to go on for ever, she wanted to stay in Joel's arms and never leave him again. She hadn't realised their desire for each other could make her so wanton, so uncaring of anything but Joel and the love they shared.

'Farrah, darling,' he groaned against her breast, his dark head even darker against her smooth creamy skin. 'God, you're lovely! Give me your lips,' he whispered urgently.

Her lips parted beneath his as he seemed to explore the very recesses of her soul. Her hands ran frenziedly over his taut back, loving the feel of his smooth, firm skin, and the way their bodies strained together in unconsummated desire. 'Joel!' she begged. 'Love me! Oh, love me!'

'I do, Farrah. More than life itself. God, you're the

sole reason I'm alive! You were born for me, made to fit into my arms, to mould against my body like the other half of myself.'

His tongue licked flames of passion across her body, arousing her to a height where she lost all reason, all will to do other than caress him back. Their clothing was a barrier she longed to remove, but at her first touch Joel drew back. He was pale, icily pale, and he moved away to sit on the edge of the bed he had carried her to.

His hair was tousled from her wild abandoned caresses, but he didn't seem to care as he made a determined effort to control his ragged breathing. The deep gulping breaths he took were long in calming and Farrah knew the willpower it took him to dampen his desire for full possession of her, for her full response to the demand of his hard body.

He picked up his quickly discarded shirt with shaking hands, standing up to rebutton it. His eyes remained averted as Farrah sat up to straighten her blouse, only looking at her when her creamy skin was again covered. 'Now you know why this has to stop,' Joel said huskily, his gaze hungry for her.

Farrah stood up to move into his arms. 'You can't mean that, Joel,' she nestled against him. 'This is just the beginning.'

Joel put her firmly away from him. 'Not just yet, we have to wait.'

'But why, Joel? Why?' Her eyes darkened with pain. 'You don't love me enough, do you?'

'What a damned stupid remark! I love you so much I couldn't think straight while I was in America. I called you because I just had to speak to you. And what do I find? Only that you've gone out with Nigel, the man you told me you were in love with. Did you lie to me about that, Farrah? Or were you just trying to hurt me?'

'I lied to you,' she admitted. 'But not to hurt you. I didn't know I had the power to do that.'

He gave a tight smile. 'You have the power, all right. I'm not altogether sure I like that, in fact, at first I really hated it. It made me rather brutal with you at times.'

'When did you know you loved me?'

He lit up a cheroot before answering her. 'I wondered when you would ask me that. I don't really know the answer. I was always attracted to you. I think I got my first jolt when you looked at me past that vase of flowers at the country house. Then that night at the club when you told me you loved Nigel I was unreasonably angry. I didn't know why, until Simon appeared and paid you all that attention. I could have resorted to physical violence when I saw you dancing with him. This might be love, but I didn't welcome the feeling into my life with open arms. But that night I had to acknowledge that my feelings went further for you than for any other woman, and in the States I had to recognise it as love. I missed you like hell!' he added fiercely.

'No more than I did you, I'm sure. Joel, did you spend the evening before your trip with Laura Bennett?'

'Is that what she told you, because if it is, then the answer is no. I just couldn't be on my own with you again before I left, I couldn't be held responsible for my actions. Then when I called you on the telephone you refused to talk to me. I was going insane over there with no contact with you at all!'

'It was the names you called me. Such hateful names.'

'Pure jealousy—the little green god raising his ugly head. I wanted to rip this Nigel apart for being with you when I wanted to be.'

'So you had him sent away?'

'Yes, I had him sent away! I wanted him removed, far away from here where you couldn't meet him. If I couldn't have you then he certainly wasn't going to, not again.'

'Not a-again? But he hasn't—he hasn't, Joel!'

'Why do you persist in that lie?' he said harshly. 'All right, you look like an innocent and I'll have to be satisfied with that. I've accepted that I won't be the first to take you. And I don't like that either, but I accept it.'

Farrah's green eyes blazed. 'There's nothing *to* accept! I haven't given myself to anyone. In my thoughts maybe, to you, but it's never been a reality.'

Joel moved angrily, marching from the room and into the lounge with barely suppressed violence. 'Stop lying to me! I have no intention of taking you yet, so your lie won't be proved or disproved for some time.'

'But it's the truth, Joel,' she insisted.

'I couldn't give a damn! You have to leave now, before I do something I'll regret.'

'Oh no. Oh no, Joel,' she gave a choked laugh. 'I won't be dismissed as easily as that.'

'I'm not doing it *easily* at all,' he groaned. 'But it has to be done. I was wrong before, you should never have been involved in this. I know Laura, I know how tough she could make things for us. And I won't have you involved any more.'

'It doesn't matter about her, as long as you want me.' She didn't like Joel like this, cold and cruel as if he were trying to drive her away. 'Don't make me go, Joel. Please!'

'What do you want me to do?' He stubbed his cheroot out viciously. 'Take you to my bed and keep you there? Because that's what would happen if I even took that delectable body of yours just once. And I can't do it. You can credit me with a lot of sins, but I'm not adding you to the top of the list.'

'But Miss Bennett's hold over you!' Farrah reminded him desperately. 'You need me for that.'

'I can't do it this way, Farrah. I'll have to find some other way out of this. I don't want the beginning of our married life ruined by her bitchiness. And we are getting married, Farrah!'

'I wasn't arguing,' she said breathlessly.

'That makes a change,' he said with a touch of humour. 'But for the moment we have to forget all about marriage plans.'

'And what do we do about our love for each other?' she asked shrilly, sensing the underlying strength of purpose about him, a steely inflexibility. 'Forget that too?'

Joel sighed. 'If you want to.'

'I want—I want *you*, Joel! I just want you in my life.'

'I want that too. I want to wake up mornings and find you there beside me, come home in the evenings and find you waiting for me, just to have you with me and know you belong to me for now and always. I want every damned bit of that. But I can wait until Laura is out of our lives.'

'I can't,' she said stubbornly. 'I don't see why we have to.'

'No, I guess you don't. You had a sample of Laura's mischief-making, do you think you could stand that for another few months?'

'I can stand anything if I know I have you beside me,' she smiled at him glowingly.

'God, I love you!' It was a groan from deep within him.

She moved back into his arms, pressing her face against his chest. 'Let me stay with you tonight,' she begged huskily. 'Just tonight.'

His hands caressed her shoulders, exploring every creamy inch of skin. 'I want to, Farrah, but I can't,' he gave a harsh laugh. 'You know, this is some sacrifice I'm making, who've always taken what I wanted and hang the consequences. But with you I want everything to be done properly, including having our wedding night as the first night we make love together. I can wait until we're married, I have to.'

'And we don't have to part now?'

Joel lifted her chin, gently parting her lips with his, pulling her closer as passion mounted between them. 'I couldn't be parted from you now for anything. You've really hooked me, little darling, whether you want me or not.'

'Oh, I want you,' she murmured huskily.

'I have something for you,' he picked up his jacket and began sorting through the pockets. 'I intended giving you this anyway, whether you decided to marry me or not,' he brought out a small square ring box, opening the lid to reveal the most beautiful ring Farrah had ever seen. A huge emerald surrounded by six diamonds set on a narrow gold band, the ring matched the bracelet on her wrist perfectly and she realised this must be the ring Joel had told her about. He lifted her hand, slipping the ring on her finger. 'This is your engagement ring, Farrah, and in my case it's just as much a committal as a wedding ring.'

Farrah raised herself on tiptoe, kissing him softly on the mouth. 'I love you, Joel.'

'And I you,' he gave a self-mocking smile. 'I must be mad, I who've always hated emotional ties, tied to a woman's whims in business and engaged to another woman.'

It was almost dark outside, the villa shrouded in the

last of the evening's glow. Farrah stood before the open french doors, watching the lap of the calm sea on the flat golden sand. Joel came to stand beside her and she turned to him, her eyes softening with their shared love. They swayed together languidly to the soft music coming fom the room behind them.

Joel nibbled her earlobe. 'You once called this making love to music,' he murmured huskily.

'I know.'

'You're completely shameless, Mrs Falcone,' he said humorously.

'I know that too,' she laughed throatily.

He pressed her possessively against him, burying his face in her neck. 'Mmm, you smell good.'

She laughed softly, her happiness almost too much to bear. 'I needed a shower after all that salt water. Oh, Joel, it's so beautiful here.'

His lips caressed her skin in soft gentle movements. 'I knew you'd like this place the moment I saw it.'

'But what a wedding present! I love you so much, Joel. Only you could have thought to give me a villa on the French coast as a wedding gift.'

Joel took hold of her hand and they walked together out of the villa and down along their private beach, the gentle breeze softly stirring their hair. The two of them bathed here in complete privacy during the day, Farrah's whole body acquiring a light golden tan. It had been almost impossible to believe when Laura Bennett had finally given in and sold Joel her shares. It had been the announcement of their engagement that had finally triggered off her wish to sell, for which Farrah felt truly grateful. Joel refused to think about marriage until he had full control of his firm, and as he also exercised full control over his own feelings the last few months had been a great strain to both of them. But that was all behind them now, and only happiness remained ahead of them.

He stopped beside the gentle lapping of the water, his harsh features softened with love for her and the true happiness they had found in their marriage. 'You're perfect, Farrah, perfect and beautiful. I couldn't believe it on our wedding night when you came to me in complete innocence. When I realised I was your only lover I wanted to get down on my knees and kiss your feet. I should have believed you, trusted you when you told me it would be so. But neither love or trust have come easily to me. I told myself that it didn't matter that there had been other men, that I couldn't expect you to have saved yourself for me. But you had! And you'll never know how humble that made me feel.'

She looked up at him with glowing eyes, her finger tips touching his parted mouth. 'I didn't want you to feel humble, Joel, just loved.'

His eyes darkened. 'But it wasn't the first time for me, far from it.'

Farrah shook her head, her lips a gentle curve. 'It doesn't matter, darling. All that matters to me is that I'm the last. I'd much rather be last than first.'

Joel turned away. 'But you should have been both! When I think of all the women I've——'

Her fingers laid gently over his mouth cut him off from further conversation. 'They don't matter, Joel, except that they've helped to make you the person you are today, the person I love, and for that I can only feel gratitude. From them you've learnt how to give me unselfish pleasure, how to excite me beyond endurance at times. None of life's experiences are ever wasted.'

'I feel—I feel so—so—— Oh, I don't know how to describe how I feel! I thought I was a hardened cynic, that nothing could touch me, and yet your lightest touch inflames me and I want you to the point of madness. Like now,' he groaned, his eyes closing as if to shut out the sight of her. 'I want to lay you down in the soft warm sand and feel your body against mine in the full beauty of your nakedness, to caress you until you cry out for mercy.'

'Please, Joel. Oh, *please*!'

His eyes darkened almost to black and he needed so second bidding as they lowered down on to the sand, their arms and bodies entwined as the last of the warm evening's light was darkened into night.

THE RIVIERA—A WORLD PLAYGROUND

Farrah and Joel spend their honeymoon at his villa on the south coast of France—most likely on the stunning strip of land known as the Riviera. Also called the Côte d'Azur, the French Riviera is a world of pleasure and privilege. Here sun worshippers lie elbow to elbow on pebble or sand beaches, the Mediterranean is an incredible shade of blue, and everywhere there are people. And yachts. And flowers. More flowers than one could ever imagine: along the roadsides, spilling over garden walls, or in carefully tended fields for the nearby perfume factories.

The Riviera's three famous playgrounds are Cannes, Nice and Monte Carlo. Cannes is the site of the annual International Film Festival, and each May the "beautiful people" flock there to see and be seen. Nice, built on the hills rising behind the Bay of Angels, boasts incredible scenery, carnivals, antique shops and even the ruins of a Roman arena. And Monte Carlo, in the independent principality of Monaco, is known for its palatial casino, the Grand Prix motor race, its impeccable style...and the storybook romance between Prince Rainier and his Princess, the former Grace Kelly.

But there's more to this narrow coastal strip, and among the most enchanting beauty spots is Cap d'Antibes, which may well be the location of Joel's villa. Jutting boldly into the Mediterranean between Cannes and Nice, Cap d'Antibes is celebrated for its splendid gardens and villas and golden beaches. Truly a honeymooners' haven!

Harlequin ◆ *Salutes...*

JANET DAILEY

...with 6 more of her bestselling Presents novels!

Once again Harlequin is proud to salute Janet Dailey, one of the world's most popular romance authors. Now's your chance to discover 6 of Janet Dailey's best—6 great love stories that will intrigue you, captivate you and thrill you as only Harlequin romances can!

Available in May wherever paperback books are sold, or through
Harlequin Reader Service:

In the U.S.
1440 South Priest Drive
Tempe, AZ 85281

In Canada
649 Ontario Street
Stratford, Ontario N5A 6W2